SAVAGE HUNGER

NEW YORK TIMES BESTSELLING AUTHOR
LISA RENEE JONES

ISBN-13: 978-1091111424

BE THE FIRST TO KNOW!

The best way to be informed of all upcoming books, sales, giveaways, televisions news (there's some coming soon!), and to get a FREE EBOOK, be sure you're signed up for my newsletter list!

SIGN-UP HERE: http://lisareneejones.com/newsletter-sign-up/

Another surefire way to be in the know is to follow me on BookBub:

FOLLOW ME HERE: http://bookbub.com/authors/lisa-renee-jones

THE PAST CRASHES INTO THE PRESENT

CHAPTER ONE

Savage

Present day—New York City

Tequila is the Mexican version of the middle finger, the perfect "fuck you" to someone you either can't kill or haven't decided to kill yet. It's liquid foreplay.

Exactly why I lift my shot glass at Adam, one of the two Walker Security compadres at the table with me, and down the booze, a wicked bite following.

"Sorry bastard," I murmur because he just took my money in a card game in the backroom of a New York City bar a few blocks from the Walker offices.

"Took my money, too." Smith, the other of the two Walker compadres, grimaces, tossing back his shot glass as well with a grimace. "Fuck, that burns." He runs a hand through his sandy brown hair, leaving it a rumpled mess. "Fuck."

I laugh a mocking laugh. "Little bitch-ass Army Ranger," I say, motioning to his hand. "Do you get pedicures, man? Because those are some soft hands you got there. A pussy's hands."

He snorts. "All you Green Berets do is blow shit up."

"Nah," I say, tracing my goatee and considering his level of stupidity, which is high. I drop my hands to the table and give in to the need to school this fool. "A Beret reckons himself a charmer," I explain. "He convinces people like you to blow stuff up while he watches."

Smith barks out a laugh. "You're a charmer? Give me a fucking break."

I lean forward and give him the cobra stare. The one I use right before I kill some asshole. "That's why I left. I like to do the killing myself. Could be you I decide to kill one day."

He laughs again and tosses popcorn in my face. "Bring it."

"And here we have the reason you both just paid me," Adam says, scooping up the pool of money. "You were both running your mouths and not paying attention."

"How about I come over there and shut your mouth?" I taunt, refilling my shot glass. "Then we'll see how Mr. SEAL Team Six does against a mercenary."

Adam's lips quirk and he leans forward, too—a big motherfucker, tall and broad, his dark hair a typical curling, wild mess. "We're all mercenaries now," he claims. "We work for profit."

"Not the way I did before I came here, and you know it." I run a finger down the scar on my cheek. "This only made me more of a bastard." I down another shot of tequila, feeling the booze when the new waitress heads our direction. She's a pretty little thing, a brunette who favors the only perfect woman I've ever known. A resemblance that might just require the entire bottle of tequila find its way to my belly. As if trying to make sure that's what happens, she kneels beside me and whispers, "A man who just handed me a hundred-dollar bill to request your presence is in the alleyway."

The hair on my arms goes all prickly. "Name?"

"Tag."

Iron Man might as well have punched me in the chest, but I don't react. "Thanks, sweetheart," I say. "Enjoy the money. You deserve it just for speaking to the prick." I reach into my pocket and palm her another hundred. "Go now."

"Thanks," she says, scraping her teeth over her bottom lip, an invitation in her eyes that I have no intention of accepting. Anyone who reminds me of *her* is a no go for me.

The waitress stands up and I don't watch her depart. I focus on Adam and Smith. "Count me out this hand," I say,

8

shrugging into the leather jacket at the back of my chair, remarkably sober considering my level of tequila intake.

"Where the hell are you going?" Adam asks, the card deck in hand. "I'm dealing."

"I'll return to win my money back in a few," I say. "You better practice while you can." I stand up, taking the Glock at my hip right along with the blade hidden inside my waistband for this reunion.

I walk toward the front of the familiar bar, where I've hung out hundreds of times in the past three years since I joined Walker Security. This place is my comfort zone, a place to relax, and because I know Tag far more than I wish I knew Tag, that is exactly why he chose it. With long, measured strides, I make my way to the front door, because fuck no, I'm not walking into an un-scouted alleyway with a bastard like Tag. I exit into a bitter November chill that has nothing on a winter I spent in Russia. Adrenaline and agitation pulse through me as I walk to the end of the street and around the corner to enter a narrow walkway side street.

I stop short to find Tag is waiting on me, exactly as I'd expected he would. "Knew you'd take the attack route."

I step toe-to-toe with the brute of a man I once considered more a father than the bastard of a man I'd called father until I figured out I hated the fuck out of him. He's older now, cigarettes and years in Afghanistan shriveling up his skin like a damn raisin. "What the hell are you doing here?" My voice is low, taut, a threat he won't mistake as a greeting.

"Good to see you, too, Savage."

"Fuck you, Tag. What the hell do you want?"

"I'm in deep shit. I need a tug out."

"Whatever, man." I turn to leave.

"You owe me. You know you fucking owe me."

I stop dead in my tracks, grimacing with those words.

"I've never asked for payment. I'm demanding it now."

I turn to face him. "You don't demand shit of me, man. Fuck you. Get one of your boys on the payroll. They're stuck suckling your tit. I'm not."

9

"Someone burned me, betrayed me. There's a hit out on me. I'm going underground until this is over. You're the one I trust to handle this."

"*Handle this*? Define that statement."

"A job you'll enjoy, I promise. I need you to hit the man who's the mastermind."

Trigger pulled. "I don't hit," I say. "Not anymore." I turn to leave him, and this shit, behind for good.

"I have so many ways to burn you and you know it."

Acid burns my chest and I stop walking, but I don't turn and look at his ugly fucking face again.

"I wonder how your past affects the Walkers' reputation," he threatens softly and it is a threat.

My hand goes to my gun and I pull the fucking thing, turning to point it at Tag, who is pointing his own weapon at me. Piece of shit. "You don't think I know you, Savage?" he challenges.

"You won't kill me. You need me."

"And you won't kill me. You don't want a mess to clean up." He holsters his weapon. "You owe me."

"To think I once respected you." I holster my weapon, aware as he is aware that a debt between mercenaries is a blood oath. The price of betraying that oath is not pleasant. "I don't do threats," I say. "I will, however, honor the favor owed. *If* I have the facts and feel good about the job. The end. My debt will then be paid. And if you come to me after it's paid, I *will* shoot you. Start talking."

"You know how this works. We protect the integrity of the mission. We cut off a leak at the knees. You go where I send you and await instructions."

He reaches into his jacket and pulls out an envelope that he hands me. "Your mission, should you so choose to take it." With that, he steps around me.

I rotate to speak to his back. "To think I used to respect you."

He glances over his shoulder at me. "I don't give a fuck if you respect me. An oath is an oath." He disappears around the corner and I stand there, fingers curled in my palms for one reason: if I move, I will kill him. I shove the envelope into my pocket and glance skyward, the dark, starless night a perfect match for my return to that man's world. I can't put off reading my instructions and even if I could, this needs to be behind me.

I yank it from my pocket again and open it to remove the white card inside with only one word, one place, the place I swore I'd never return: San Antonio.

"Damn it to hell," I growl, squeezing my eyes shut, the torment on Candace's face when I told her I was leaving gutting me in ten different directions.

I ball up the paper, tossing it against the wall.

A movement behind me sets me off and I whirl around, grab the asshole sneaking up on me, and shove him against the wall.

"Holy hell, Savage," Adam growls. "What the hell is wrong with you?"

"Why the hell are you ghosting me?"

"I know you, man. I knew there was trouble. And I saw who you were talking to. He's that piece of shit you were working for when we met, beneath you a hundred feet. Whatever he wants, you're saying no."

"You don't make that decision." I release him and step back, scrubbing my jaw. "I'm off the books for a couple of weeks." I rotate away from him and exit the alleyway.

I've made it three steps when he's by my side. "San Antonio? You've got to be kidding me, man. I know what that place is to you."

"You don't know shit."

"Candace. Your father."

I stop walking and turn on him. "How do you know about Candace?"

"Vodka, man. I told you to stop drinking it. You forget when you drink vodka."

"I don't talk about Candace."

"Yeah, man. On at least three occasions. Which says a hell of a lot about why you're single."

"You're single, too, you prick."

"Your point? Never mind. My point—"

"Unless it involves more tequila, I don't care." I turn and start walking. He falls into step with me. He's pissing me off. "Get out of my face, man. I'm a live wire right now, and it has nothing to do with you. Don't make it about you."

"Punch me, asshole. Whatever. You go to San Antonio working for that asshole, I go with you."

I flag down a cab, and when it screeches to the corner, I climb inside. Adam follows. "Airport," I order.

The driver guns the engine. I open my door and tumble out onto the road, leaving Adam prisoner to speed. I'm on my feet and down a side street, fast-tracking into a subway tunnel before he can recover. Once I'm on a train, it's done. Adam is out of the picture. I just saved him from putting himself on Tag's radar. The way I tried to save Candace from me. And yet, here I am, on my way to San Antonio, and if Tag even thinks about involving her in this, I won't just kill that little prick. I'll make him suffer.

SAVAGE AND CANDACE

THE PAST, THE BEGINNING

CHAPTER TWO

Candace

Ten years ago—San Antonio, Texas

The rain cloaking the roadway, an unyielding curtain blinding my vision. This was not what I had in mind when I left my empty little cottage in Alamo Heights to head to my favorite late-night study spot. I wanted to snap out of my blurry-eyed haze and just finish the design work I'm doing for my internship, not die when my car careens into the ditch. I'm blessed to have acclaimed architect Wesley Miller mentor me, and I'm determined to prove it has nothing to do with his brother working underneath my father's military command. I'm going to earn this. I'm going to make my parents, and myself, proud of my work.

I just—I can't be home right now without thinking about my mom. Not when my home was inherited from my grandmother two years ago, and now my mom is gone, too. And of course, my father deploys to Iraq next week. I just need noise around me, anything that keeps me focused on it and my studies.

Thankfully, my destination, a place called Halcyon, where coffee and spirits are available until two AM, is a mere one block down. I hope. I think. It's hard to tell right now. Peering through the darkness, I cruise by the driveway and make a quick turn into the parking lot. Thunder erupts overhead, jolting me, but I remain focused on my goal: parking and just getting into the warm, dry building. Considering the sea of cars present, all of which are all but floating, I'm shocked to eye a few open spots near the door.

Luckily, I whip into the great spot and kill the engine. I glance at the clock and eye the ten o'clock hour. I have four hours to caffeinate and stuff my face with a piece of chocolate ganache cake. I deserve it for surviving this past month. I won't sleep much if I stay until closing, but I wouldn't sleep anyway. A man rushes from the front door of the coffee bar and hurries to the vehicle next to me, wasting no time speeding away. Considering the rain has now become a monsoon, that works for me. I grab my umbrella and shove the door open wide, giving myself room to open it, grab my briefcase, that doubles as a purse, and step out into the storm.

In a rush of shutting the door of my Ford Focus and locking up, I finally step inside the warehouse-style operation, with high ceilings and two levels. I set my umbrella by the door and maneuver through the clusters of wood and steel chairs, with random cushy chairs here and there as well. I place my order, scanning to find one spot, one last table by a window where I can keep an eye on the storm. Claiming the small table, I reach in my bag for my drafting pad and grimace. It's not here. Please tell me it's in the car. I grab my wallet and stuff it in my pocket, along with my keys, leaving my bag to hold the table.

Hurrying back outside, I'm relieved to find the rain has slowed to a light drizzle, though I don't trust that it will last. I pull up my hood, rushing outside to watch an SUV park so close that I can't even get into my car. The asshole opens his door and I've had my limit. I charge toward him and by the time he's standing I'm on his side of his door with him.

I don't even care that he's taller than any man I've ever actually stood this close to and as broad as the doorway. I'm pissed. I'm hurt. I need an outlet and he just made himself that outlet. "What are you doing?" I demand.

He yanks down his hood, displaying a handsome, sculpted face, with dark hair mussed up in that "finger fucked by some gorgeous woman" kind of way.

"Staring at a pretty lady, it seems," he says, his voice a low, whiskey-roughened rasp, and yet somehow as deep and big as the man.

I ignore the compliment and the purr of my body, a reaction that I attribute, not to his degree of hotness, which is scorching, but to my lack of male companionship in far too long. "I can't get into my car. You parked on top of me."

"You parked over the line and I didn't want to get my pretty little head all wet."

"I didn't park over the line."

"You did," he assures me. "Go look." He motions toward my car. "I'll wait here."

"I'm not going to look. You have to move. I can't open my door."

He crosses his arms over his impressively broad chest and peers at me from under dark, intense brows. "What are you going to give me if I do?"

"How about I save your manhood from my knee?"

He laughs, a masculine rough laugh that may as well be bedroom talk for the way my nipples respond. Good Lord, what is wrong with me? I don't know this man. I do not *want* to know this man. My nipples do not get to know this man. "How about," his gaze lowers to my mouth, lingers there and lifts, "you have coffee," he pauses for effect, "with me."

My stomach does a little flutter that I shove away, replacing it with a far more appropriate response: disbelief. "Are you seriously bribing me for entry into my own vehicle?"

Thunder roars above us and the rain begins to plummet down again. To my shock, he catches my hand and suddenly I'm pressed to his hard body, his hands on my waist. My senses blaze in a wildfire of reactions, and just that quickly, he's lifted me into his vehicle, out of the rain. Instinct has me scooting to the passenger door, which is of course, right on top of my car door. I couldn't escape if I wanted to, and suddenly, he's inside the cabin with me, shutting the door.

CHAPTER THREE

Candace

"What are you doing?" I demand indignantly, my heart beating like a hammer in my chest. "You can't grab me and throw me in your vehicle."

He turns to face me, the small cabin made smaller by the massive size of this man. He's just so *big* and close, so very close and I can smell his cologne, something woodsy with a hint of amber. My senses are on fire. *Wild fire.* I can't think straight. "I was saving you, woman," he replies. "It's a mad downpour out there. But if you want me to let you out, I will."

Thunder crashes again and I jump, eyes squeezing shut a moment, then lifting to find him staring at me. "Well?" he challenges softly.

Well indeed, I think. How did I end up in a vehicle, in a storm with the hottest man I've ever seen?

"You're still an asshole."

"Does that mean the fair maiden wishes to remain in the shelter of my fine vehicle?"

"I should be afraid of you right now."

He arches one of those dark brows again. Why do I think his brows are sexy? Brows are not sexy. "Are you?" he challenges.

I blink. "Am I what?"

"Afraid of me," he supplies.

Oh, that. His brows distracted me. "I should be," I repeat.

"Why are you out at this time of night alone?"

"Why are you?" I clap back.

"Why not? Who do you think a bad guy would attack? You or me?"

"Depends on which one of us has the biggest gun."

He laughs that hell of a sexy laugh again that my nipples still find a bit too sexy. "Do you carry?" he asks.

"Yes. And I know how to use it," I add, because I do. Of course, my gun is not present on my person, but I don't point that out.

"You're a fierce one," he comments.

"You're an arrogant one," I say in rebuttal.

"I'm not arrogant," he says, his energy darkening, his mood a swift, stormy shift. "A smart-ass, yes. Arrogant, no."

"Parking too close to me wasn't you being arrogant? Just a smart-ass?"

"Yep." He grins in my direction, his mood drastically altered. "How'd I do?"

"Perfectly."

"Glad to hear it," he says. "I'm Rick Savage, by the way, but most people call me Savage."

"They call you Savage? Are you supposed to be making me feel better?"

"Savage can have many meanings, sweetheart," he murmurs, his voice low, suggestive, and the obvious insinuation that he's a savage in bed has my cheeks heating.

He chuckles. "Shy, are you?"

"I'm—not actually. Not really."

"You did come at me like a freight train, I'll give you that. Call me Rick." He offers me his hand, a strong hand that I'm now imagining on my body again, but this time in the most savage of ways. God. I don't know this man and I'm fantasizing about him.

I steel myself for the impact of touching him and press my palm to his. Heat rushes up my arm and my gaze shoots to his. "Candace Marks," I say softly, but when I try to pull back, he holds onto my hand.

"Nice to meet you, Candace," he says softly, his eyes warm on my hot cheeks.

"I'm not sure if it's nice to meet you or not yet, Rick."

His lips curve and I find myself thinking about that kiss, about his mouth on my mouth. I tug at my hand and reluctantly, it seems, he releases me, or perhaps it's me who didn't really want him to actually let go. Until now, until this night and my encounter with Rick Savage, I didn't realize how much I just need to be touched. Afraid I'm transparently desperate, I turn away from him, watching as rain transforms to hail plunking on the window. "What brings you here so late and in a storm?" he asks.

I shift to face him again, happy to be back on safe territory. "School and work."

"What are you studying and/or working on?"

"Architecture. I'm interning right now under a rather famous architect. It's a bit intimidating, but exciting."

"Interesting choice of career. What do you want to build?"

"Everything. I have so many dreams. The tallest building in the world that reaches well into the clouds. The most unique building in the world. The most secure building in the world. The most impressive homes on planet Earth."

"That's what I call passion. Are you following in someone's footsteps?"

"No. I think it started with a fascination with the pyramids and morphed into architecture. What about you? Why are you here late at night?"

"Med school. I'm a surgical resident at Fort Sam where my father's an instructor."

"Impressive. It is, after all, considered the most important military medical training facility in the world. My father's at Fort Sam, too, but he's not part of the medical division. He's the commander for the North. Are you military?"

"I am, in fact, military."

"Our fathers might know each other."

He gives a nod. "I'm certain they must."

"I thought soldiers were pack animals and yet you're here, alone. It's dangerous out alone, you know," I tease.

He doesn't laugh. He cuts his stare and grabs the steering wheel, his powerful forearm flexing with the tightness of his grip. "Sometimes alone isn't the best place to be." He looks at me, his eyes swimming with something I can only call dark and damaged before he asks, "Now is it?"

I don't know if he intends for me to actually answer that question, but I do. "No," I say. "No, it's not." And then before I can stop myself, I add, "Especially not tonight." A confession, perhaps inspired by the hint of understanding between us that I believe he's trying to confirm.

"Why not tonight?" he asks.

"You don't know me. You don't need to pretend to care."

"I don't pretend. *Ever.* And as for barely knowing each other, we are the freest we will ever be together. You don't have to choose to see me again. You don't have to think about the mistakes we've made together. You don't have to do anything, including answering my question." And yet he asks again, "Why not tonight?" he repeats.

I exhale a shaky breath, my fingers twisting in my lap, my gaze shifting forward to the window drizzled with rain. The storm outside has calmed, but the one inside me has not. "My mom died last month. My dad is deploying to Iraq next week." I glance over at Rick. "If that's not enough, I live in a house I inherited from my dead grandmother who I loved very much."

"Do you have a boyfriend, Candace?"

"No. I mean, I did, but it wasn't serious. He was military and a little too busy trying to impress my father for me to feel like anything was about me. What about you?"

"No one."

No one.

There is something hollow in the way he says this that only drives me to want to know more. Turning his prior question, back on him, I ask, "Why are you here alone, Rick Savage?"

He fixes me in a deep blue stare, and I swear I'm drifting in a sea of this man's making. "To meet you. I just didn't know it yet."

The rain explodes around us again, an eternal roughening of the windows that only Texas does with such force. Thunder erupts with it, lightning in the distance, and

I don't know who moves first. Him or me. Suddenly though we're in the middle of the seat and his fingers are tangling all rough and wonderfully in my hair, his mouth lowering to mine. "I'm going to kiss you now, unless you object," he says.

"Kiss me already, Savage."

"Rick. Call me Rick." And then his lips collide with my lips, his tongue a deep stroke of pure heat that has me moaning with the rush of sensation that assaults my body in the best of ways.

My arms slide around his muscular back, body pressing against his body, the hard lines of this incredible man absorbing more than the softer part of me. That need to be touched explodes inside me, demanding satisfaction. He pulls back and stares down at me. "Do you want to get out of here? Together?"

I tell myself this is crazy, insane, wildly out of my character. "I don't do things like this. Ever."

He kisses me again and leaves me breathless. "Then make me the first."

CHAPTER FOUR

Candace

Then make me the first.

Those words linger between us, my decision ending this encounter with Rick Savage, or making it last all night. My hand flattens on his chest, over his heart, and the thundering of his heart beneath my palm, the absolute proof that he's all in, pushes me over the edge. "Yes. Yes, I want to go with you."

"I don't live far," he says. "Do you want to follow me or get your car in the morning?"

"My place," I say quickly. "Can we go to my place?"

"Of course." He strokes my cheek. "Do you—"

"I'll ride with you," I say because I just don't want to ruin this vibe between us, whatever it is. And I don't want the chance to talk myself out of this. "But I need to go inside. I left my bag and my order."

"I'll go, but I also need to move your car. You really did park like shit."

"I did not park like shit."

He laughs and kisses me. "You did. Let me have your keys."

I dig in my pocket and hand them over. "How are you and your big body getting in that door?"

He scoots back to his spot behind the wheel and turns on the engine, cranking the heat and then backing up the vehicle before pulling us into the next parking spot. "Like that." He winks. "I'll be fast." He yanks up his hood, opens the door, and then he's gone, shutting me inside in a wake of that delicious, woodsy cologne of his.

I scoot forward, trying to spy him through the rain, but he must walk around the back of the SUV because, in a flash, he's beside my window, climbing into my car. He backs it up, and it, right along with the man, disappears. A minute later, he's obviously parked it nearby because he's already at the door of the coffee bar. He enters and disappears inside. My god, my heart is racing all over again. There is something about this man that I can't explain. Something mysterious. Something broken. Something I can't turn away from. *He'll hurt me*, I think. Broken people hurt other people, but I can't seem to care. It's not like I'm going to fall in love. I'm just going to fall into him for one night.

I wait for his return and wait some more. I could almost believe he left, except that I'm in his vehicle. Maybe he hopes I'll leave? No. That's silly. The connection between us is real. You can't imagine this kind of heat. I sink back into the seat and press my hands to the leather, my heart pitter-pattering as fast as the rain hits the window, my nerves keeping pace. What's taking so long? The door opens and there he is, a big and devastating man standing there, holding my bag. He shoves it behind the seat and then rejoins me, offering me a coffee cup. "I had them remake it and," he sets a bag down next to me, "they boxed up your cake. I got a slice for me, too."

I blink. "You had them remake my coffee?"

"It was cold." He shuts the door.

My body burns for this man, but the thoughtfulness in his actions warm me from the inside out. "Thank you."

He cuts me a sideways glance that sparks with all kinds of sizzle. "You have to share."

"I do believe you earned half the coffee."

He smiles and faces the window, shifting us into reverse, pulling out of the space and driving us toward the exit.

I sip the delicious white mocha drink and then, once we're on the road, and with a flutter of my stomach, I offer him a drink. "Share, right?"

"Exactly," he agrees, accepting the cup. "It' sweet," I warn.

"The sweeter the better," he assures me, taking the cup and giving me another wink. "Where are we going?" he asks, taking a sip.

"Alamo Heights," I say, heat burning low in my belly with his lips on my cup, where my lips just were, too. "Lamont Avenue."

"I know exactly where that is."

"You do?" I ask, surprised.

"I don't live far," he explains. "My father owns a bunch of real estate from back in his days in private practice."

"He was in private practice?"

"He was a plastic surgeon. He *is* a plastic surgeon. He made loads of money and then had a car accident that damaged his hand." He takes another drink and the intimacy of sharing my coffee with Rick somehow feels more intimate than a one-night stand. So does the conversation.

"That's horrible."

He sips again. "Good stuff," he says of the coffee, offering it back to me, and the minute I take the cup, he pulls me closer, aligning our legs. "Don't feel sorry for my father. He's an arrogant prick."

"But you're not?"

"Let my actions speak for me. You'll have to decide for yourself."

I like this answer. I like it a lot. It's the kind of answer my father, who I respect immensely, would give. And I wonder if I will ever know Rick long enough to discover his real self. "I will," I say, sipping the coffee.

We don't speak again. We just share the coffee, our hands brushing, our lips touching the same place on the plastic lid, our legs connected, the air charged with our attraction. Once he's turned onto my street, I direct him to the cute little cottage that is my home and use the clicker on my keychain to lift the garage.

Rick pulls his SUV inside the garage and kills the engine. That's my trigger. Nerves explode in my stomach. "I, ah—"

He leans in, his hand on my face. "We can talk. We can finish that cup of coffee. We don't have to do anything else."

"You came for more than coffee."

"I could call a half dozen women and get fucked. I didn't come here to get fucked."

The bold words shock and thrill me, softening the wall I didn't realize I'd erected inside me. "Maybe you're not such an asshole after all," I whisper.

"I can be," he admits, those perfect lips curving as he adds, "but I do believe you've proven you can swat me into place."

"Rick," I whisper.

"No one calls me that. You know that?"

"Savage—"

"No," he says quickly. "*Rick.* I like how it sounds when you say it. I like it a hell of a lot."

Those words hint at that dark torment I've sensed in him before now, something he chooses to let me see. Something that makes him human in all the right and wrong ways. My nerves fade into something I can't even name. Want. Lust. Need. Understanding. I grab the lapel of his jacket and whisper, "Rick," before I press my lips to his and let him know that I need to be kissed. I need to be kissed by him.

CHAPTER FIVE

Savage

The minute Candace's tongue touches mine, my resistance is shredded. I kiss her. I kiss the hell out of her, breathing her in, consuming her the many ways she's consuming me. I went to that coffee bar to get out of my house, to get out my head, and I found *her*. She moans into my mouth and I reach for the door, opening it, sliding out of my Pathfinder and taking her with me. I turn her and never let her go, molding her close, kicking the door shut.

The coffee goes flying, crashing to the ground. "Oh crap," she murmurs. "I can make more and—"

I kiss her again because I can't stop myself. I wanted out of my own head tonight, and she's that escape. I can feel the push and pull inside me that led me to no place but her. I can feel the dark hunger for more growing inside me. I brush the hair from her face, tilting her gaze to mine, and I hide nothing from her. I let her see every cutting, dark edge that drives me this night. I let her see what is there, let her have the chance to run. "If I go inside right now, I'm not going to stop kissing you."

"Good," she whispers.

That's all I need to hear. I kiss her again, drinking her in, the sweet, delicate taste of her that is still somehow wild; inhaling the floral scent of roses lifting off her skin and her hair. God, I want to be lost in this woman and I want to do to it now. Scooping her up, I carry her toward the door, where I set her down in front of me, facing the door, my hands on her hips as she fumbles with her keys and drops them. I lean down and scoop them up. She turns to face me, and when I straighten, her hands settle on my chest.

"I really don't do this kind of thing," she says. "*Ever.*"

The vulnerability in her, the nerves, jolts me with a shot of reality. I don't know Candace. I don't know why I want to know her so damn badly, but I do. And that means this can't be about my wants and needs, or my shit day and life. Not right now.

"My father wouldn't approve," she continues, "and that shouldn't matter, but—"

I cup her face and bring my lips almost to hers. "We'll talk," I say, the words about killing me, my cock all but busting my damn zipper, but I mean them. "Just talk," I add. "And eat chocolate cake. I told you—"

She presses her lips to mine and I force myself to grab the edge of the door, not her, when it's her I want to touch. When it's her I want to feel all sweet and submissive against me. Her I want all over my hands and tongue, her riding my cock. But that's not all this is or I wouldn't be here right now, not with Candace, not knowing what she's going through. And so, I resist what I want, replacing it with what she needs. She'll tell me, she'll show me what she needs.

Her hands slide over my body and my fingers curl around the doorframe. "You're killing me, woman. I'm trying to be a gentleman."

She presses into me, her body aligned to mine. "Don't. Don't be a gentleman. I wasn't saying I want to talk. I just want you to know that you're not just someone to fill a void tonight. It might seem that way, but—but please *don't* be a gentleman."

I catch her head with my hand. "Do you want to talk or fuck?"

"Can we do both? Is that a problem?"

She's so damn sweet and adorable. And beautiful. The kind of woman I don't deserve, but typical of the Savage men, I'm too selfish to care tonight. "Both works damn fine for me." I kiss her and open the door, turning her toward her house.

She flips on a light, the way she's flipped me inside out. I don't fuck and talk. I just fuck and move on because that's all I have to offer, but I can't seem to remember that with Candace. I can't seem to fight the urge to see and know more about her. Shyly, it seems, she catches my hand and leads me inside to a kitchen, a long, rectangular-shaped room sporting a long, shiny, white counter. A counter I consider setting her on top of and fucking her right here, right now. Then we could talk and fuck some more. She shrugs out of her coat and I do the same, both of us hanging them on a coatrack just inside the doorway. I'm back to considering all the ways I could fuck her on the counter when she catches my hand again and drags me forward and into a cozy little living room that fits her perfectly. A typical unnecessary Texas fireplace is the centerpiece of the main wall, framed by navy blue couches and chairs. She leads me to the couch and sits down, setting her purse on the table. The minute I sit, she twists to face me. "I have wine," she offers, her voice trembling. "I'll grab it." She pushes to her feet, intending to walk away.

I'm on my feet, catching her tiny waist before she has the chance. "I don't want a drink." My hand slides under her hair, resting on her neck. "I want you."

"Yeah?" she asks softly.

"Yeah." I sit and take her with me, rain roughing up the roof, echoing in the hollow of a home that reminds her of loss tonight. This grounds me. This reminds me that her actions tonight are driven by that hollow she wants to fill. The same way I want to replace the noise in my head with her soft moans. I won't regret that tomorrow, but she may. I slide my hand to her leg. "You were close to your grandmother?"

"Very."

"And your mother?"

"Very." Her eyes gloss over. "She was an officer in the Army." Her voice cracks. "There was an accident."

Her pain punches me in the chest and I bring her fingers to my lips. "Military is a rough family gig."

"That's why you don't have to worry about me falling for you. I *can't* do the military thing. I won't. In other words, I'm a safe escape."

This news should deliver relief, and with any other woman, it would do that and more. With any other woman, it would be a ticket to fuck and leave. Instead, I roll her to the cushion, onto her back, and I follow her with something completely different on my mind. "I'm going to change your mind."

"You don't even know me."

"I *want* to know you," I say, and I can't even believe how much I mean these words. I don't do relationships. Life has taught me they don't work. They punish you. They hurt you. The way my father hurts my mother, but I can't help myself with this woman.

"Why?" she whispers.

"Because everything about you feels better than anything else." My hand slides under her shirt and my mouth closes down on her mouth, tongue stroking against her tongue, and damn, she's sweet, so *damn* sweet. I deepen the kiss and her fingers twine in my hair, a soft little moan sliding from her mouth to mine.

That's when the doorbell rings. I pull back and stare down at her, wondering if this is some other guy come to make her feel better. "Expecting someone?"

"No. No, I have no idea who would be here in this rain." She scoots up to a sitting position and grabs her phone from her purse. "My security system is on my phone." She punches in a few keystrokes and her eyes go wide. "Oh God. It's my father. He's waiting on the porch."

Her father, who she's already told me won't approve of me being here.

We both sit up and she twists around to face me. "I don't want you to leave," she says. "So it's on you now to decide what comes next. Stay. Go. Hide. Meet my father. What's it going to be, Rick Savage?"

CHAPTER SIX

Candace

I don't want Rick to leave, but of course, he will. Why wouldn't he leave? He barely knows me, and my father, the five-star general, is here. Rick stands up and takes me with him, sliding a hand under my hair to my neck and kisses me hard and fast. "Go let your father in. I'll make a pot of coffee."

I blanch. "You're going to stay?"

"We haven't talked, fucked, nor have I convinced you to see me again, so hell yeah, I'm staying."

I blink in surprise. "You know you want to see me again?"

"I just told you I'm going to make you fall for me, baby. I can't do that and not see you again."

"I thought you were just talking in the moment."

"I don't say shit to get laid. That's not who I am." He strokes my hair. "Go get your father off the porch."

"It's covered."

"You're the only one who needs to be wet tonight." My cheeks heat and he laughs. "Go get your father." He kisses me. "I'll make that coffee." He rounds the coffee table and walks toward the kitchen, this big, gorgeous man I barely know daring to stay and face my father.

He can't know what that means. "Rick!" I call out.

He turns at the entryway to the kitchen. "Yeah, baby?"

God, why does him calling me baby do such crazy things to my stomach? "He's a five-star general who protects his daughter."

"Good. He should." And with that, he disappears into the kitchen and my stomach is fluttering all over again. Oh God. He's already doing it. He's making me want to like him. He's making me want to see him again.

The doorbell rings again and I head toward the front foyer, promising myself that no matter what happens with Rick Savage, I will not fall for him. I open the door. My father's standing there in full uniform with a box in his hand. "Your favorite chocolate cake. Millie made it."

Millie being his housekeeper, who I've known most of my life, and who I both love and adore. "It's crazy outside and it's late," I say. "I can't believe you brought it by tonight. Come in, dad." I back up and he enters, pausing to kiss me.

"I want as much time with my daughter as I can get before I deploy."

He enters the house and I shut the door, only to find him charging toward the kitchen. "Any chance you have coffee made?" he calls over his shoulder.

"Dad!" I call after him urgently, my heart lurching. "Dad!"

He ignores me and I rush after him, only to hear, "And who exactly are you, young man?"

"Dad," I pant out, catching up with him and grabbing his arm. "This is—"

Rick salutes my father. "Sir."

My father stares at Rick. "At ease, son. You're military?"

"Yes sir," Rick confirms, but he doesn't offer his name.

My father glances at me. "Something I need to know?"

"He made coffee," I offer.

"Should be done any minute," Rick adds, standing tall and straight, allowing me the ability to fully appreciate his size and physical condition, which is as stunningly tip-top as it gets.

My father sets the cake on the counter by the fridge and then steps across the kitchen to the end of the counter where Rick is monitoring the coffee pot. They are now face-to-face as my father asks, "What's your name son?"

"Rick Savage, sir. My father is—"

"I know who your father is," my father snaps back. "And you aren't dating my daughter."

I gasp. "Dad! What are you doing?"

"His father—"

"Is a prick," Rick supplies. "An arrogant prick. What does that have to do with me?"

My father doesn't miss a beat, still on the attack. "Born from the same blood, son."

I tug on my father's arm, but he won't look at me. "I can't believe you're doing this, Father."

"It's okay," Rick says, but he doesn't look at me. He remains focused on my father. "With all due respect, sir, you don't get to decide who your daughter dates."

My father's temper snaps in the air, a live charge. "You underestimate my wrath if you believe I can't control you seeing my daughter."

Most men would cower, but Rick doesn't. "If you judge me by my father," he says, "and in turn dictate to your own daughter what she can and cannot do, your adult daughter, I might add, then perhaps the real problem here is how much *you're* like my father. In which case, I'm more determined to be in her life than ever because she needs me."

No one talks to my father like this and I'm now officially terrified that Rick is going to be punished. "Dad, please. I beg—"

"Don't beg," Rick says, his gaze falling on me. "Ever, to anyone. Do you want me to leave? Because if you do, I will, but I don't *want to* leave."

"No," I say quickly. "No, I don't want you to leave."

He gives me a nod and meets my father's stare. "She gets to judge me by my actions, not my father's, and decide if I belong in her life. Not you. You don't get to judge me."

A muscle in my father's jaw flexes, tense seconds ticking by before he asks, "What do you do for the military, Rick Savage?"

"Surgical resident at Fort Sam, under my father."

"You want to be like him?"

Rick's expression doesn't change, but there's a sharp charge to the air around him. "Never will I ever be like that man."

"But you want to be a surgeon?" my father pushes.

"Should we go to war, should *I* go to war, I will save our soldiers and I will kill our enemies, so in answer to your question: yes, sir, I want to be a surgeon."

My father's eyebrows jump up, which, no doubt, is my own reaction. "And fight? You want to fight?" my father asks.

Rick doesn't even hesitate. "Abso-fucking-lutely."

That reply twists me in knots. "Well, there you have it, dad," I say. "You can stop judging him. That answer is the reason he and I are just friends." Tears burn my eyes just thinking about my mother's accident and my father's deployment. "I need coffee and cake." I walk to the counter opposite both men, open a drawer, and grab a fork. I then remove the top of the box my father brought, expose the yummy-looking chocolate cake and fill my fork with a giant bite. I shove it all into my mouth.

Savage and my father appear on either side of me. Savage takes the fork from my hand and then scoops a bite of cake that he too shoves in his mouth. He used my fork in front of my father. It's this intimate, assuming act that says we're as intimate and as assuming as the action. There's a message in the action. That message is his rejection of us being just friends. "Damn good," he murmurs, his eyes warm as he hands me back the fork.

"I can't," I whisper, certain he'll understand my meaning. I can't fall for him.

"Challenge accepted," he replies.

"Let me get a bite of that cake," my father says, opening a drawer and then producing his own fork, claiming a general-sized bite of cake. "Hmmm," he approves. "Millie is damn good."

Rick arches a brow at the comment that means nothing to him. "Millie's been his housekeeper since I was a kid," I explain.

"Your mother loved this cake," my father says, and then quickly clears his throat, a hint of emotion there he doesn't hide. "I do believe we all need plates and that coffee." My father rotates and walks to the cabinet behind us.

Rick wipes my lip and licks the chocolate off his finger. "I like it even better now." His eyes twinkle with mischief.

"You're bad," I whisper.

He leans in close and whispers. "Only as bad as you let me be."

With that, my nipples are puckered, my thighs pressed together, and all while the hottest man I've ever known is a few inches from my father, the man I admire the most in the world.

A few minutes later, we are all in the living room, listening to the rain hitting the rooftop while eating cake and drinking hot coffee, the conversation turning to my father's favorite subject: *football*. One it seems Rick enjoys as well. It's not the night that I'd envisioned at all when I went to the coffee bar. It's not the night I envisioned when I brought Rick home. It's something much better.

My father doesn't linger once the cake and coffee are gone, and it's not long before I walk him to the door. "I'm glad you're not alone," he says softly. "I just don't want you to get hurt."

"I'm not going to get hurt, dad."

"If he hurts you—"

"I'll deal with him, not you."

His lips thin. "He seems like a good man. Better than his father."

I lower my voice. "What *is* the scoop with his father?"

"He's got a God-complex and that's bad news. It gets people killed. It also could be very hard to live with. I get the feeling your young man has lived that hell." He kisses me. "Call me tomorrow."

I nod and shut the door, wondering about how hard it was for Rick to grow up with his father and now to work underneath him. That darkness I've felt in Rick, the torment that I've tasted in his kisses, now has new meaning. He's not here to spend a night with me and walk away. He proved that when he stood his ground with my father. But I have to walk away. I can't fall for this man. I can't. Not a soldier. My heart can't take it.

With this in my mind, I hurry back into the living room where Rick sits on the couch. I step in front of him, towering over him. He doesn't react by standing, by trying to claim a dominant position. He doesn't get up at all.

"I need—" I say, my voice trailing off, my thoughts tumbling into the mesmerizing deep blue sea of his potent stare.

He leans forward, his hands settling firmly, possessively, on my hips, his touch weakening my knees. "What do you need?"

Him, I think. I need him and nothing else. I need to be lost. I need to escape. And I think he needs the same. That need drives me to be daring, or perhaps it's this man who drives me to be daring. That darkness in him is loneliness. He's alone. I don't know how I know this, but I know. And I don't know where this leads—I suspect heartache—but tonight, he's not alone. Tonight, he's wanted and needed and I intend for him to know this without question.

I tear my shirt over my head and toss it aside, my bra following, the air between us charging with instant sexual heat. His eyes rake over my body, appreciation in their depths, but when I climb onto his lap, straddling him, he is not wicked and wild. He is not all about sex. He's tender and gentle. His hands slide over my body, up my back and he whispers, "What if I never let you go?"

I know this is a moment of passion, a question not to be taken literally, but when Rick Savage kisses me after he speaks it, when he drinks me in and makes love to me with his kiss, it's hard to want this to end. And it's easy, at least for right now, to hope he doesn't ever let me go.

38

THE PRESENT

CHAPTER SEVEN

Savage

Present day—San Antonio, TX

San Antonio might as well be a third-world country. It's hot as fuck, the mosquitoes are the size of birds, and my bastard father lives here. On the plus side—it does have plus sides—the eating is damn good, and the Mexican food comes with all the "fuck you" tequila you can afford. And she's here. Candace is still here, which I know because I've made sure I know. I've kept tabs on her location when I've wanted to keep tabs on a whole lot more. But I didn't. I couldn't, and so I stayed away. Just the idea of her hands on another man's body, and his on hers, is still, to this day, enough to drive me fucking nuts.

But here I am, in her place, her city, and that isn't an accident. It's by way of obvious design. Me, her, my past, and this job, all collide in one way: Tag. Tag chose me for whatever the hell this hit is because he knew he could use Candace to control me. I'm no fool. That means whoever I'm supposed to hit is going to be a problem for me. A big fucking problem.

My chartered plane hits the runway in Texas at three in the afternoon, the day after Tag fucked my life ten times over. It took that long to book the plane under a fake businessman, a millionaire asshole named Steve Winter, just one of the many identities at my disposal thanks to Walker Security. I then rent a high-end BMW under the same fake name. The one I choose doesn't matter. That it's untraceable does. Not that this hides me from Tag, who'll be watching Candace, waiting on me to find her, too. No, the

41

name isn't about Tag at all. It's about sheltering myself from the hit itself.

I drive the black beast of a machine straight to my old stomping grounds, registering at Hotel Emma, a five-star joint a few blocks from Candace's neighborhood. My neighborhood, too, considering I lived with her for a year. The best damn year of my life. I open my suitcase and remove a Glock and shove it into the back of my pants, under my shirt. A Ruger goes under my black jeans and inside my boot, a blade inside my second boot. I grab a thin black jacket from my bag, that despite the wicked-fast approach of the holiday, really isn't needed, but it's better camouflage for that Glock than my shirt.

My cellphone rings with Blake Walker's number. I scrub the rough two-day stubble on my jaw and sit on the kickass bed. "What the fuck is going on? I know where you are and what name you're using. Start fucking talking and tell me why you've gone rogue?"

"I'm doing clean-up," I reply, sitting down on the bed. "The kind that you can't afford for me not to do."

He knows what that means. He knew the risk of my past when he brought me on. And all he says is, "What do you need?"

His loyalty leaves me with only one answer. "For you to stay the hell away so this doesn't touch you." I hang up and head for the door, listening to my gut that brought me to Alamo Heights. Candace is my weakness and apparently so was thinking I could drink vodka around Tag or he wouldn't know Candace still matters to me. Staying away from her to protect her no longer works.

By the time I'm in my car, starting the engine, I've worked through the decision I've wrestled with the entire flight here. I could play this coy and hide my intentions to protect Candace. I could pretend she doesn't matter and hope that tricks Tag into believing he made a misjudgment. I could, and perhaps I should, but Tag's too good and runs too sophisticated of an operation for that to fly. And he'll know what I know. I'm the most dangerous when I'm in your face, pissed the fuck off. I'm going to go straight to Candace and tell her everything like I should have a hell of a long time ago, but first, I need a plan that doesn't freak her the fuck out as much as seeing me is about to freak her the fuck out. One that doesn't put her on the run for the rest of her life or bury her six feet under.

That means I need to see her father, who loves the fuck out of his daughter, who I have far more of a history with than Candace knows. Or maybe she does. I have no idea what the fuck her father told her about me or the history we created after I left Texas. But that history included Tag. He'll understand that Tag means trouble. He'll understand that he's now in the line of fire with me, right along with his daughter. That talk needs to happen now, and if I'm lucky, considering it's Sunday, he'll be at home watching football. If he's not deployed.

It takes me all of five minutes to pull into the neighborhood that still owns a piece of me because Candace still owns so damn much of me. Gut-wrenching memories batter me. The night I met Candace. The night I met her father. The day I said goodbye a year and a half later. I punch the steering wheel and turn into the drive of the sprawling white mansion where Howard Marks, her father, lives. I'm here to set-up my first "fuck you" to Tag, of which there will be many and soon. I'm not sure how her father will react to seeing me, considering our complicated history, but fuck it. I charge up to the door and ring the bell. I wait. And I wait some more. Impatiently, I knock. No answer. Damn it. I scrub my jaw and march back to my car. Fuck it again. I'm going to do what I really want to do anyway. I'm going to see Candace.

Just the thought has adrenaline pumping through me like I'm in a damn warzone. Fuck. She hates me. I don't want her to hate me. I slide into the BMW and play every possible reunion in my mind. None of them end well. I pull into the drive of her cottage, the one her grandmother left her just two years before we met. All I can think about now is seeing her, kissing her. I need to kiss her again, just one more time before I die. And I'm not sure when I do if I'll be able to walk away.

I walk to the door when I want to run and break it down until she's in front of me and in my arms. My finger punches repeatedly at the bell for a reason. She hates when people do that. She'll rush to the door and I'll pretend that it's me she's rushing to greet. Me that she can't live without. Me that she loves. Instead, I brace myself for the hate.

CHAPTER EIGHT

Savage

The hate doesn't come.

Candace doesn't answer the door. I knock. I knock again. No answer. Damn it, she must be with her father. Out of patience, I drive a few blocks to the strip mall where her best friend Linda owns a floral shop, parking right at the front door. Linda will know where she is. I walk to the door, pull it open and find Linda, a pretty, petite blonde, holding an armful of lilies while talking to an elderly woman. The minute Linda spies me, her eyes go wide.

"You," she bites out and the next thing I know she's standing in front of me and the flowers are flung at me, a small hint of what I might expect from Candace. The flowers don't hurt, but the emotion beneath Linda's action is a blade slicing me open. I hurt Candace and I hurt her badly or Linda wouldn't be this upset. "Why are you here?" she demands.

"I need to see her."

Her jaw sets hard. "No. No, you don't *get* to see her."

"I still love her." The words roll off my tongue without an ounce of hesitation.

She points a finger at me. "You don't get to love her. Ever. You left."

"I didn't have a choice. I was deployed."

"And never came back. You sent her a Dear Candace letter."

"I had no choice," I repeat. "I was protecting her."

"From what?" she demands.

"Bad people."

45

"I don't know what that means," she says. "What does that mean?"

"It means I was protecting her, and damn it, I cannot leave this earth without kissing her one last time."

She snorts. "She's engaged. Her future husband is rich, good looking, and present. Do you want to take that from her?"

Engaged.

I could double the fuck over. Somehow, I stay standing.

"Oh God," Linda whispers. "You really do still love her."

I don't even care what she just saw in me to draw that response. "Every day of my life," I assure her, the stabbing pain of her engagement not going away. "Every day."

"Then why did you leave?"

My fingers curl in my palms. "I told you, I had no choice." I turn and head for the door, shoving it open, a bar and some of that Texas tequila in my sights.

"She doesn't love him."

At those words shouted by Linda, I stop dead and rotate. "She's fucking marrying him." I don't wait to hear her reply. I know Candace. She wouldn't marry someone for anything but love. I'm a fool to have thought that she did anything but bury my memories. It's been too long and I did her too fucking wrong. I turn and start walking again and this time I don't stop until I'm inside that bar, ordering that "fuck you" tequila. "Just bring the damn bottle."

The bartender arches an eyebrow. "The bottle, son?"

"That's right, old man. The bottle. Got a problem with that?"

He grabs the bottle and sets a shot glass in front of me, filling it to the brim. I down the contents.

"I'll take a glass to go with that bottle."

At the sound of Adam's voice, I turn to find him sliding onto the stool next to me. I scowl my worst scowl, the kind of scowl that makes lesser men run for their lives. "You little prick," I say, about as loving as I ever get these days. "What part of 'stay the fuck away' do you not understand?"

He doesn't run. He smirks and motions to the bartender. "Where's that glass?"

The bartender sets a glass down in front of him and pours the tequila to the brim. Adam downs the contents and then grabs the bottle to refill our glasses. "Drink," he orders. "We get along better when you're not a whiny little sober bitch."

"I should kill you for that." I down my shot.

"Bring it," he says. "I'll give you a scar on the other cheek."

"That's your wet dream, right? The idea that you might actually be able to beat me in a fight."

"Shut the fuck up and drink," he orders.

"Only because I want to," I say, downing my shot.

Half a bottle later, I want to punch someone or something, an invisible knife carving out a piece of my heart. "She's marrying another man," I murmur roughly. "She deserved better anyway. She's getting it."

Adam arches a brow. "You sure about that?"

"Come on, man. I was a piece of shit before you and Walker found me."

"You thought you were killing bad guys," he says, justifying for me. "We wouldn't have brought you into Walker if we didn't believe that."

"I didn't care who I was killing or I would have figured my shit out sooner. I was a cold motherfucker."

"Cold motherfuckers don't wallow in tequila over the love of their lives." He doesn't give me time to reply, adding, "What are we doing here, Savage?" He pokes the bar. "Right here where the only woman I've ever heard you talk like she mattered lives."

"Apparently, she's marrying that other guy while I protect her so she can do it." I grab the bottle and take a slug all direct and shit.

"Why did he bring you here, man? Why does Tag want you here? I need to know what we're into."

"I owe him a favor. One more hit and he'll leave Walker the hell alone."

"You aren't that fucking gullible. You don't believe that shit. There's always 'one more.' He'll keep coming at you and he'll do it over and over and over again."

"Yup. That's why I have to kill him and all his compadres."

"Alone?"

I love this bastard. He doesn't say: no, you can't kill them. He just questions me doing it alone. "You think I can't?" I challenge.

"I think you have a woman on your mind, and her being here, where this 'one more' hit is, isn't an accident. That's what Tag wanted. For you to be distracted. And come on, man, what are the odds this is some random hit that just happened to be here?"

"I assume he thought of me when he found out the job was here."

"Or it's something else. You're being set up."

"Maybe," I concede. "But I've been out of this shit for years."

"It's like the damn mob and you know it," he says. "You don't get out. Not alive."

A commotion sounds behind us and then a woman shouts, "Stop!"

Grimacing, I turn around to find a guy groping her. I scowl. "Hey, man, stop that shit."

"Fuck you!" the guy yells back at me and his three big buddies all turn in our direction.

The first guy grabs the girl's breast, right in front of me, a dare for me to come stop him.

She punches him and tells him to stop. I don't react and neither does Adam. Not just yet.

"Stop that shit!" the bartender yells at the man. "Or I'll call the damn police."

The woman screams at the man and I don't even have to turn to look at him. I stand up and take another drink directly from the bottle. "Call them," I say. "I'll hold down the fort until they get here."

"Oh hell, here we go," Adam murmurs, pushing to his feet and dropping a black American Express on the bar, shoving it at the bartender. "Charge the damage to that card."

The bartender's eyes go wide and I laugh. "Don't worry. We won't kill them. We'll just make them look stupid, but you have a job, too. Get the girl out of here." I twist around and charge toward the men lurking and waiting on us, only to have a big football player bastard charge toward me, a pool stick in his hand. Oh yeah. Bring. It. On.

I step into him and just that fast, the stick is in my hand, not his. I break it in half and the dude lunges at me. He ends up under my foot and flat on his stomach. The woman runs past me while another asshole charges in my direction. Adam intercepts, grabbing him and in about thirty seconds he's taken the asshole and hung him by his belt loop on one of a number of hooks on the wall. That's about when the entire bar of a good fifteen patrons breaks into war. It's me and Adam against them all and I have some fun, but these boys are not warriors. They're boy scouts with wedgies up their arses. They're no challenge, and too soon to see that change, sirens screech and police charge into the bar. Tequila roughens up my mind but not enough to make me stupid. I don't even think about fighting the men in blue. I turn and let one of them cuff me. I got no beef with the cops, but they damn well should with me.

Adam steps to my side and offers the same cop his hands as well. "Happy, man?" he asks me while metal clamps his wrists.

"Not even close to happy," I assure him. "We didn't finish that bottle."

The bartender steps in front of us and motions to the cop. "These two were saving a woman those men were manhandling. And they even paid for the damage to the place in advance."

"They're still coming with us," the cop, a thirty-something redheaded linebacker of a dude, crankily snaps before he points toward the door. "Both of you walk."

I stumble forward, perhaps feeling a bit of that tequila, but I'm not its bitch. It's my bitch. "We need that bottle on the bar," I say, eyeing the officer over my shoulder. "We paid for that."

49

"Just keep walking," the officer says, nudging me forward.

"Holy hell, we don't even get to finish the damn bottle."

"That's because you couldn't just wait on the cops," Adam says as we step into the dimming sunlight. The heat is still suffocating as fuck, too, a cluster of wimp-ass bar patrons, who couldn't fight worth a shit, being shoved into random cars.

"Your ass didn't wait either," I say. "And you didn't want to wait." I eye the officer. "She was being groped," I say as he grabs Adam and walks him to the other side of the car.

"*Rick*. Oh my God. Rick?"

At Candace's voice, my heart freezes in my chest. I turn around and there she is, Candace is standing right here, all but in front of me. And God, she's beautiful, her long, dark hair cascading over her shoulders. Her green eyes are like green grass on a perfect summer's day, but they're flecked with amber in anger. Her pale skin flushed red. "Why are you here?" she demands.

"Holy hell, woman. I need to kiss you." I take a step toward her.

The cop punches my arm and forces me back, and of course, I could go through him and I'm thinking about it, but Candace handles him for me. "John, damn it, step back!"

The redhead, John, I guess, backs off and I don't like him. "You know him? You fuck him, too?"

She slaps me. "What right do you have to even suggest who I did or did not sleep with?"

I glare at the cop. "Did you fuck her?"

"Stop, Rick!" Candace shouts at me. "Stop now."

Rick.

That's what gets me. Her calling me Rick. No one but her calls me Rick. My gaze jerks back to her beautiful face. "I need to talk to you. *Fuck*. I need to kiss you. Do you know how long I've needed to kiss you again?" I step toward her again and John grabs me.

"Let him go, John!" she orders, pointing at him and then me, and to my surprise, she closes the one step left between us and pokes my chest. "What are you doing here?"

That poke isn't just a poke to me. This is her hand touching me when I have lived a decade waiting for just that moment. My voice lowers, the tequila evaporating. "I need to talk to you."

"You wrote me a Dear Candace letter. You *broke* my heart. You hurt me. *Go away* and just let me try to move on."

She wants me to let her *try* to move on. That means she *hasn't* moved on. "I didn't," I say. "I didn't move on. I have never moved on from you."

Her eyes meet mine, searching my face, the million right things about us in the air, alive and well, but the one thing that went wrong is so fucking there, too. The one thing that destroyed us is not only right here between us, the hurt I made her feel isn't even close to gone. And bastard that I am, I can't be sorry. Because fuck her fiancé. She's hurting right now because I still matter to her.

"Go away," she whispers again and then with a stronger voice she adds, "*Savage.*"

Savage, not Rick. I turn my cheek as if I've been hit again and she walks away, but not before I get a view of her cute little ass in a black skirt. That ass that belongs in my hand because she belongs in my arms. I'm not done looking when the cop shoves me toward the open car door and I slide in beside Adam. The door shuts behind me and Adam says. "Rick? You hate Rick. No one ever calls you Rick."

"Except when she calls me Rick," I say, glancing over at him. "That went better than expected, don't you think?"

CHAPTER NINE

Candace

I'm shaking so hard I can barely stand up, but somehow, I shove open the door to Linda's flower shop, the bells chiming loudly with my abrupt entry.

"Candace," she gasps from behind the counter where she's helping a customer. The gasp, no doubt, because I don't do abrupt and intrusive like I am right now. I'm polite. I'm proper. I'm a five-star general's daughter. I also just slapped the only man I've ever loved while he was in handcuffs. Today's that kind of day. I'm pissed off among many other emotions I'll deal with later.

"Why didn't you warn me?" I demand. "Why did you call me over here for something important, which was obviously him, and not warn me?"

The woman standing at the counter turns to face me, her freckled face reddening. "I'll ah, give you two a few minutes." She rushes in my direction and behind me, the chimes telling me she's exited, not likely to return and I don't care.

"Why didn't you warn me?" I repeat.

Linda rushes around the counter. "Because this is the kind of emotion the man you marry is supposed to make you feel."

"Pain? Heartache? Hurt? That's what the man I marry is supposed to make me feel?" I demand.

"Passion. Love. Investment. You two were young. He went off to war. He saw things. He did things you and I can't fathom. And he's here now. Talk to him. Just talk."

"You don't understand what you're doing right now," I all but scream at her. "You don't understand."

"I know this is the most emotion I've seen from you in a decade."

I can't speak another word or I will lose my shit as if I haven't already. I rotate and launch myself toward the door. "Let's go to the bar and have a drink," she calls out. "We can talk and—"

I whirl on her. "Rick just turned the bar into a warzone. We can't go and have a drink there. And I don't want to go have a drink with you anyway."

"Because I told him you're engaged. That should tell you where his head and heart are right now."

I don't say another word. I leave and once I'm in the BMW that I worked my ass off to buy while Rick Savage was nowhere in sight, I grip the steering wheel. He's not just going to rip my heart out again. He's going to end up shattering my world in ways he can't possibly understand.

Savage

I'm leaning against the cell wall a foot from Adam when the doors open. "About damn time we get our one call, John. Dear John, the little prick," I snap at the sight of the asshole. "I bet it is little, too."

"Could you shut up for ten seconds?" Adam asks, pushing to his feet while I do the same.

"I didn't fuck her, man," John says. "I worked for her father."

"Where *is* her father?" I ask. "I need to speak to him."

"Deployed," he replies, "which is in your best interest. You're free. You're out. Get the hell out of my face before I punch you for her." He leaves the door open and walks away. "Both your cars were impounded," he calls over his shoulder.

Adam and I share a look. "Did we call Blake and I don't know it?" I ask.

"We did not," he says. "Which lends to the question: who got us out?"

Tag, I think. Tag got us out because Tag wants me to do his dirty work.

A few minutes later, we have our personal items back on our persons and Adam calls for an Uber. "I'm at the same hotel as you," he says. "Surprise."

"Just what I need," I reply dryly. "A pain in my ass right next door."

"I, am, in fact, right next door," he assures me.

"Fan-fucking-tabulous. The only thing I'd like better is a bottle of pickle juice waiting for me on ice in my room. Then my life would be made."

"Figures," he says. "You are a sour puss and all."

"Better than a pussy, which I am not."

"Maybe if you were just this once," he suggests dryly, "we wouldn't be leaving jail right now."

"Whatever."

We exit into what is now the ten o'clock hour and there's not a breeze in sight. It's hot. It's humid. It's fucking Texas calling me a little bitch. We cut left to the parking lot and that's when I spy Candace, standing in the parking lot beside her car. "Maybe Tag didn't get us out after all."

"I didn't know that we thought he did," Adam replies. "But I'm taking it the pretty brunette is your love?"

"She damn sure isn't yours," I snap. "And since yeah, she obviously got us out to see me, show your appreciation by getting lost. I'll catch my own Uber."

"We still haven't talked about Tag."

"Buzz off," I say, breaking away from him and striding toward Candace, who doesn't move. She just hugs the hell out of herself the way I want her to hug me. Now. I want her to hug me now.

My steps widen, quicken, and I don't stop until I'm in front of her. I do, however, intend to stop there, but her sweet floral perfume, so damn familiar and addictive, undoes the fuck out of me. So does her backing up like she's scared of me.

I catch her arm and then step all the fucking way into her, my fingers diving into all that silky hair, my mouth capturing her mouth. She gasps, her hand on my chest where she clearly intends to push, but that doesn't happen. My tongue strokes deep, caressing against hers, her soft body hard with resistance for about ten seconds. A soft moan slides from her lips, one part frustration, another part something raw and hungry. And then she's kissing me back, her fingers curling into my shoulders, body arching against mine. My hand slides between her shoulder blades, molding her close, holding onto her and she holds onto me, too. It's like coming home, like part of me has been missing, like every hole I've filled with the wrong women and too much booze is now filled with her.

A siren sounds, and that's how this ends, at least for now. Candace shoves back from me. "Stop. Stop right now."

Damn it, I can't ignore her telling me to stop. I know this, but I can't let her go again. "Come back to my room with me. Let's talk."

"Like you just *talked*?"

"We, baby. That wasn't just me."

She shoves her finger with a rock the size of Texas on it between us. "I'm engaged to another man. We have nothing to talk about."

"You didn't kiss me like you were engaged to another man. You kissed me like you wished he was me."

She starts shoving against me. "Go. Leave. Get back."

My jaw clenches and I step back. "Did he find that little sweet spot of yours? Because I'm better, or you wouldn't have just kissed the fuck out of me."

She points at me, her cheeks rosy, her hand trembling. "You don't get to come back here and talk to me like that. Ten years, Savage."

"Eight, and it's Rick to you."

"I came here for one reason. To tell you to stay away forever this time." She walks around the car toward the driver's side door. I want to pull her back. Fuck. I want to throw her over my shoulder, tie her up, and force her to go to my room.

I pursue her and when her door is open and she's about to climb in the car, I am right there in front of her. "I'm not going anywhere but to my hotel room, *alone*, where I will think of your mouth on my mouth and my mouth on your body. I'll also be contemplating how many ways I can get rid of the asshole who put that rock on your finger." I turn and start walking away.

"Maybe you can kill him," she calls out. "Because you're a mercenary and a killer, right, *Savage?*"

I stop walking, grinding my teeth with the knowledge that she knows my past, that her father probably tracked me down. I turn and face her. "I was, in fact, those things and more, but that's not the reason your fiancé should fear me. The way you just kissed me. That, he should fear."

CHAPTER TEN

Savage

I call the rental car company, give them my credit card, and arrange for another car to be delivered to my hotel room, which they claim will be within two hours. In the meantime, I'm walking down the side of the road when a car pulls up next to me and the window to the backseat rolls down to display Adam. "Get in."

I eye the Uber sign on the window.

At least the driver ensures Adam can't nag the fuck out of me, plus it's also hot as balls, which doesn't work well with blue balls. I need a cold shower before my new rental car arrives. During that shower, I'm going to think about what comes next, which somehow, someway, will include Candace naked and in my arms. The car door pops open and I slide inside next to Adam, my knees at my damn chest. "Could you get a smaller fucking car or what?" I eye his knees at his chest. "We look like we're trying out for a bad porn movie."

"I don't even want to know what's in your head to come up with that comparison," Adam says dryly. He taps the driver's seat. I shut the door and the vehicle starts moving. "How'd that thing you just did go for you?"

"Better than expected," I say again because I kissed her. And she kissed me the fuck back like she couldn't kiss me long enough or hard enough.

"That's why you were walking?" he challenges.

"I'm not under her car with her wheels on my chest," I comment dryly. "Baby steps."

"I hear she's engaged to another man."

"Not for long," I assure him.

"Because you're going to do what?"

"Get rid of him."

"That may not be as easy as you may think."

I glance over at him. I don't ask what he means. I was a fucking paid mercenary and she's the angel that I have always known deserves better than the devil I've become. But devil that I am, I can't seem to care anymore. Not after I tasted her again. Not after I touched her again. I have to have her. She *will* be mine again.

Adam's phone buzzes with a text message and I don't miss the tightening of his expression. The car pulls into the hotel driveway and we exit the vehicle, walking past the doorman and into the fancy lobby. "What was that shit you were talking back there?"

He glances over at me. "Research Blake did on Tag and your old flame." We round the corner to the elevator and he jabs the button. "You want this to end well?" he challenges. "You need to hear me out and you need us in on this."

The elevator doors open. "I don't know what the fuck you think you know," I say, stepping inside and using my keycard to punch in our floor. He joins me and the doors shut before I add, "But you don't know enough or you wouldn't have made that ridiculous, kindergarten version of a hero's statement. Walker isn't the answer to everything."

"You'll rethink that when you hear what I have to say."

I smirk. He smirks. We stare at the doors, waiting to get to a place free of cameras and recording devices. The elevator door opens and we walk straight to my room. Without a word, we both start a search for listening devices, meeting in the living room where we sit down on the couch.

The minute we're clear, I go on the attack. "Walker can't be involved in my dirty business or they become dirty."

"Do you think I, or any one of the three Walker brothers, are stupid?"

"Stupidly loyal."

"And you're a stupid fool if you think you get out of this with that woman and your life without us." He doesn't give me time to cut him down with words or punch him, for that matter, which is my preferred attack. Comes from being a surgeon's son. I know how to use my hands, and I know how to use them to save a life just as well as I know how to end a life. "Do you know who Candace is engaged to?" he asks.

I snort. "I don't give a fuck about who he is."

"Considering why you came here in the first place, you should."

I cut him a look. "What the hell does that mean?"

"I think you know what it means. We talked about this already. But just in case the tequila clouded your brain, I'll repeat: you. Her. This place. This hit. None of it is an accident." He grabs his phone and punches a few keys. "His name is Gabriel Manning. He's a Texas Senator. Rumor is that he's positioning himself for a 2024 run for president." He offers me his phone.

I don't take the phone. I scowl, another thing I'm good at. Killing and scowling rank high on my list of ways I prove that I'm charming. "What the hell are you talking about?"

"He's the former Associated Deputy Director of Military Affairs for the CIA, now a U.S. Senator representing Texas, who apparently knows her father well. Do you know where I'm going with this?"

I scrub my jaw. CIA with a connection to Candace's father and as it seems, Tag. And he's a high-profile asshole running for office. The picture is crystal clear. He's the reason I'm here. He's going to be the hit. He's going to be the man Tag expects me to kill. *Holy hell.* He said I'd like killing this one. He wasn't wrong.

"What are we into, Savage?" Adam asks, and the question snaps me back to reality.

"*We* aren't into anything. You need to get out of this now."

"You think her fiancé's your target."

"We aren't talking about this. I'm going to take a shower." I walk around the table toward the bathroom.

"What if he's a good guy?" he demands. "You can't just kill him to save her."

I stop and turn to face him. "If you'd seen the CIA do what I've seen the CIA do, you wouldn't want him to breathe another day."

"We have Walker family that's ex-CIA," he argues.

"And I don't work with them for a reason. I'm damn sure not letting one of them marry Candace."

"What if she loves him?"

"She doesn't."

"She's engaged to him," he reminds me.

"I told you. *Not for long.*" I turn again, but there's a knock on the door.

"What if this is what Tag wants?" he challenges again. "For you to kill a good man because this is personal to you."

I turn to face him. "You think my woman ended up engaged to a man who Tag wants dead and that's a coincidence? I didn't know SEALs were that stupid."

"By that logic, he can't be the hit at all. Maybe you just want it to be him. Because he has her and you don't."

My jaw flexes. "You need to leave before I hurt you."

"Come at me, man," he says, motioning me forward with his hands. "Better you come at me than him before you know what you're dealing with. Blake is looking into his history. Give us time to figure out what this is."

"I don't know how many ways to say this, but I don't want Walker involved. You consider that maybe that's what this is? An attack on Walker, using me to get to them?"

"I think this is about you. You don't walk away from a man like Tag, knowing where to find his dirty laundry. Maybe Tag watched your woman, and you, and looked for an opportunity to take you down. Maybe he thought this would be easy. Maybe he thought you have no fucking control. Maybe he doesn't want to end you or us. Maybe he wants you to believe you belong with him because you're no better than him."

I laugh. "You're such a damn drama queen."

"You want her back. Win her back. Killing him means you think you aren't good enough to win a battle of the heart."

"Now you sound like a Hallmark movie."

"I've seen you watching Hallmark movies," he counters.
I smirk. "Only if there's nothing else on, asshole."

"And the ones with dogs. You like those."

"Shut the fuck up," I snap. "I know what you're doing. You're trying to make me more human than I am."

"You think 'Savage' wins her back? You think killing the competition wins her back? I heard her use your name, man. I saw the look on her face when she slapped you. You're going to have to be Rick."

"Same man, different name," I say, but in my mind, I can hear her saying, "Maybe you can kill him. Because you're a mercenary and a killer, right, *Savage?*"

"Wait, what look on her face?" I ask.

"Fear," he says. "She still loves you and it scares the hell out of her. You scare the hell out of her."

And there it is. The reason I had to walk away from Candace, simplified down to basics when my reasons were far from simple. But at my core, I didn't want to see fear in her eyes when she looked at me. I didn't want to deserve that fear. And I *do* deserve that fear, from everyone else but her. Tag better fucking fear me because I'm going to kill him before this is over. But *not from her*. I will die for her. I will protect her. I will do whatever it takes to keep her safe, even if it ends me in the process.

CHAPTER ELEVEN

Candace

I loved Rick Savage. I loved him so damn much that he was a part of me, one half of my soul. He owned my heart, which I gave him freely. And then he left and never came back. I waited and waited. I prayed for him to return. Then I prayed to stop caring. I failed on that and failed brutally, but still, I gave up on him.

I spent years of my life hurting over that man and finally I convinced myself that I didn't really feel all those passionate, intense things I'd thought I'd felt for him. It was all a façade of memories gone wrong: a fairy tale I'd created in my mind that never existed. And then he showed up today, acting like he's what I've been waiting for and all those passionate feelings showed back up with him.

That man destroyed me and now he's about to take all that there is left of me, all that I care about. He can't be here now. He will take all I have left and leave me to bleed out.

I pull into my driveway, hit the garage door opener, and wait impatiently for the door to rise. Anger burns through me, the safest emotion I dare allow myself until I'm alone, and perhaps, ever. It controls me, a fierce live charge that has me driving far too quickly into my garage and slamming on the brakes. My black convertible BMW, my gift to myself when I watched the final brick go up on my first commercial design, jerks to a stop, and I hit the button to seal myself inside. The car I bought to celebrate alone. Savage was gone. My father was gone. There was no Gabriel then. I had no idea what a blessing that was, either. Me and men don't work.

A mental flash of that first rainy night with Rick has me killing the engine and opening the door before I dive down a rabbit hole that I've been trapped inside far too often the past decade of my life. By the time the garage is shut, I'm out of the car and inside the house, locking the door behind me. I don't stop there, either. I do what I always do when I'm stressed. I pour a glass of wine and I walk to the bathroom, deposit my glass and my purse on the counter, and then start a hot bubble bath.

I've just stripped and slipped into my robe when my cellphone rings. I want to ignore it, but with all that is going on right now, I can't. I yank it from my purse and find Gabriel's number. God. *Not now.* I don't know how I play this role I've chosen right now, this night when I'm dealing with the emotional impact of seeing Rick. But I have to. I have to or bad things might happen. I force myself to answer. "Hey," I say, my voice cracking. God, my voice cracked. He's going to notice.

"Just wanted to make sure you got a dress for tomorrow night," he says.

Not hello. Not how are you. Not hey honey. He's worried about me being arm candy at a political fundraiser. At least he didn't notice my state of mind. "I'm just going to wear something from my closet."

"No. No, I told you, you *must* stun at this event. I need you looking like a future first lady."

And of course, that takes work for me. That's clearly what he's telling me. "I'll find something."

"It's tomorrow night." He sounds exasperated.

"I know. I'll find something."

"I'll have a stylist meet you at the mansion tomorrow. I may or may not be back from Austin when you arrive. I'll text you the details of the stylist's arrival. She'll pamper you."

The mansion being the insanely extravagant home that he inherited from his father before I ever met him, which is also where he has his offices. "Thank you. That sounds lovely."

"Anything for my future wife. You know that. I'm headed to drinks with an important donor. I'll see you tomorrow."

"Yes. See you tomorrow."

He hangs up and I do what I never do. I down all of my wine when a sip is how I drink. I then pin my hair up, strip and climb into the tub, turning off the water and sinking low. Just that fast, I'm back in the past, my father and Rick eating chocolate cake in my kitchen, the only two heroes I've ever known by my side. I want to be back there again. I want to be in that moment and have everything happen differently afterward.

My cellphone rings again and I grab it from the sink to find a New York number. I don't know this number and considering I'm currently under contract to design a military facility that's had more than a few challenges, I have to answer. "Candace Marks," I answer.

"Candy."

The voice and the nickname crush my chest with emotions. There's a joke behind that name. A dirty, funny, intimate joke that shreds my crushed, torn, bleeding heart. "Rick," I whisper.

"Not Savage?" he challenges softly.

"I told you—"

"I'm not going away, baby."

"Ten years," I say, my voice lifting. "It's been—"

"Eight years, three months, and four days."

The answer stuns me and my eyes pinch with tears I've somehow fought back until now. "Too long."

"Yes," he agrees. "Too damn long. I need to see you. I need to come over."

"No. I won't let you in."

"I *need to* see you."

"I can't," I say without further definition. I can't so many things right now, I add silently.

"You can. We can. And I damn sure want to. *You* want to."

"No," I lie and tell myself it needs to be the truth. He hurt me. I can't trust him. He's trouble when I've got enough trouble right now. "No," I repeat. "I do not want to see you."

Anger rises hard and fast. "You left. You didn't come back. You hurt me." God, why did I admit that yet again?

"I did all of those things. Guilty as charged, but I also carried your picture with me every day. Every time I thought the end was here, I thought of you, and I had a reason to stay alive. I never stopped loving you. I never stopped needing you."

My throat tightens. "I don't believe you."

"Meet me somewhere if not there," he says, his voice low, rough, and with it, a ball of tightly contained emotions storm inside my empty soul and explodes as he adds, "I'll make you believe me."

"Why would I believe you? Why would I listen to you?"

"Because of us," he says simply as if it explains everything and there was a time when it would have. Now just isn't that time.

"There is no us."

"After that kiss, we both know that's a lie."

"That kiss meant nothing."

"Then I guess I'd better make the next one count. I'm not going away. *Ever* again. I'll see you soon, baby." He hangs up.

I drop my phone over the edge of the tub to the ground, stabbing fingers into my hair, tears streaming down my face. I'm a prisoner to two men. I'm in love with a man who I should hate. God, I still love Savage. I've always loved him. And I'm not only engaged to another man who I don't love, but I can't escape him, for reasons I can't tell anyone. Rick could make everything explode in my face.

He has to go away and he has to do it now.

CHAPTER TWELVE

Savage

I end that call with Candace and step into a cold shower to cool my hot body and hotter temper.

I'm not leaving. She thinks I am and I've earned that expectation from her, but I'm *not* leaving. I'm not walking away from her ever again. Considering who I am and what I've become, maybe that's selfish—it *is* selfish, but I don't even fucking care anymore. I love her and she's not better without me anymore than I'm better without her. I don't know why she's with this Manning asshole, but it's not love or she wouldn't have kissed the hell out of me tonight, all desperate and hungry. There's something off about her engagement, something wrong that's bugging the fuck out of me. I'm going to find out what, too, and if this connects to Tag, he better hope he finds God because the devil will find him. And that devil will be me.

By the time I'm wrapping a towel around my hips, I'm ready to go to her house and find out what. If he's there, well, we'll get the confrontation coming over with sooner than later.

I exit the bathroom, fully expecting to be alone, only to find that Adam's not only still here, sitting on my couch, Smith is sitting next to him. "What part of 'stay the fuck out of this' do you two fucktards not understand?" I walk to the bed and grab my bag. "Be gone when I'm back and have my clothes on."

"You naked is a good way to get rid of us," Smith snaps.

"I've seen worse," Adam replies. "There was this old lady with sagging skin in Afghanistan. I walked into the house

69

and she ran right out of the bathroom, naked as the day she was born. Scared the fuck out of me."

"Aren't you just funny as beans in a belly?" I snap.

Smith smirks. "You say the stupidest shit, Savage. Like telling us to leave."

"How's this for stupid?" I challenge. "If you're still here when I come back out here with my clothes on, I'll shoot you both." I walk into the bathroom, throw on sweats and a T-shirt, and sneakers, and then exit to find them both sitting there.

I scrub my jaw. "Fuck. You're really going to make me shoot you? At least order a damn pizza. I need the energy to shoot you both."

"Already ordered a half dozen," Adam says. "Figure we'll need food and this to get through the night." He sets a bottle of Johnnie Walker down on the table. "We need you a little drunk and chilled out before we go through all the data Blake sent our way on Gabriel Manning." There's a knock on the door. "That'll be the pizza now."

"I got it," Smith says, pushing to his feet and walking to the door.

I grab my MacBook from my bag and then sit down in a chair next to Adam. "How much dirt has Blake found on the shithead?"

"None," he says. "You know his campaign slogan?"

"No, I *do not* know the fucktard's campaign slogan."

"*Honest Gabe,*" he says. "A play of Honest Abe."

"Give me a fucking break," I murmur. "He's ex-CIA and a politician. He's not got an honest bone in his body."

"What if he does?" Adam asks again.

My jaw clenches. "Don't start with that shit again or I will carry your ass out of this room."

"You can't just kill him," Smith says, setting the pizza boxes on the coffee table. "Even if that was an acceptable answer, which it's not, your cover is blown. You did that the minute you showed up and got arrested."

"And he's a senator who's engaged to your ex," Adam adds. "You're an ex-mercenary. You'll be hunted for the rest of your life. Kidnapping works the same way."

"And then you'll go to work for Tag again," Adam adds. "Seems like we might have nailed his plan."

I open the top pizza box and grab a slice. "If I choose to kill Honest Gabe, he's dead and I won't go to jail for killing him."

"And you think killing him wins Candace back?"

"Undetermined." I motion to the whiskey bottle. "Start pouring."

"What the fuck does undetermined mean?" Smith asks, grabbing a slice of pizza.

"Tag assumes I'm like him," he says. "Apparently, you do as well, but that's another bitch move we'll talk about later. Back to Tag. He assumes I kill when someone is in my way."

I finish off my slice and Adam offers me a glass of whiskey. "I know that's not who you are. I'm just making sure *you* remember that's not who you are."

I accept the glass and down the contents. "I know who I am. I also know that I killed because people got in *his* way. I just didn't know it, which would make killing Tag my absolute fucking pleasure."

Adam fills all of our glasses again. "Tag's going down," he says. "I think we can all drink to that."

We toast and down our whiskey before I say, "Candace's father is the one who pulled me into Tag's operation," I say, admitting what few know. "I can't just take down Tag without the risk of taking down her father. I have to kill him and most of his men. That's why you boys need to go home."

"Holy fuck," Adam grinds out. "Does Candace know her father's involved with that slimeball?"

"Nope," I say, grabbing the bottle and refilling my glass. "And she can't know. What started as a legit black ops, off the books but legit, government operation that went south when a new administration cut the budget. He got out. I didn't."

"So where does Honest Gabe fit into all of this?" Smith asks. "Was the CIA a part of the black ops project?"

"There is the question," I say. "Were they, and was he? I can't, in fact, confirm CIA or Honest Gabe's involvement, but is either possible? Hell yes, it's possible. I saw a shit-ton of CIA bullshit during my Tag years. And I killed a few of those dirty bastards."

"*Were* they dirty?" Adam asks. "Or did he convince you they were dirty?"

I don't hesitate on that one. "I take killing our own seriously. The ones I killed, fuck yes. They were dirty."

"And now one of the high-level ex-CIA bastards is engaged to your ex-fiancée," Adam says. "I don't like where this feels like it's headed. What better way to get at you and Candace's father than to go after Candace herself?"

"Playing devil's advocate here," Smith says. "What if Honest Gabe is honest and a good friend of Candace's father? What if they want to take down Tag before the election? What if they're somehow plotting against Tag? Who better to kill her fiancé than you? No one would suspect anything but jealousy."

I grab the bottle and take a swig straight up and with good reason. In that scenario, Gabriel Manning is a good guy about to marry my woman. A good guy who might be trying to save her father. That means I'd have to save Gabriel Manning, right along with Candace's father. I reject that idea as quickly as I consider it. I don't care how much time has passed; I know Candace. I know when she's happy, and she's not happy. She's not engaged to the love of her life, or even her hero, not yet at least, because that's me.

I'm the guy who's going to save her and her father. I'm her hero.

Too fucking bad she thinks I'm a monster killing machine.

Too fucking bad she's right.

I open my MacBook and then I key up the files Blake has sent me, pulling up a photo of good ol' Honest Gabe, a blond guy with a sharp nose and a sharper jawline. Bastard might be a little good looking, too. I stare at him and wait for recognition that I don't find. I've never met him. I down another slice of pizza, reading about his awards and accomplishments. Fuck. Fuck. Fuck him. Fuck me. I grab the bottle of Johnnie Walker. "Get your own," I say, standing up and heading to the bedroom where I sit down in a chair and down a slug of whiskey before I scroll through more of this Gabe fucker's history. On paper, he's perfect, but I'll know the truth when I look him in the eyes. It's time he and I meet, and after a quick scan of his press schedule, I decide the fundraiser he's attending tomorrow night is the night.

I set my computer aside and stand up, walking into the living room. "Time to get pretty, boys. We're going to a party."

CHAPTER THIRTEEN

Candace

Rick is back.

I wake to the memory of his kiss and his hands on my body, my thighs slick, nipples puckered. Lord help me, I'm having a wet dream about my ex while engaged to another man. Of course, I hate that other man the way I should hate Rick. I do hate Rick. What am I thinking? Of course, I hate him. He's an assassin who killed people for a payday.

Throwing away the blankets, I quickly dress in leggings and a tank, heading for the door for my morning jog that is often my only version of sanity. Stepping to the porch, I draw to a halt as I find Rick standing there holding two Starbucks cups, his dark hair cut short. His black T-shirt is pulled snug across an even more impressive chest than I remember. But it's the sunlight cutting down the scar on his cheek that has my attention, that has me wondering who cut him. It has me wondering what hell he's lived through and why he chose it over me.

"Peppermint mocha," he says, my gaze jerking to those rich, deep blue eyes of his as he adds, "your favorite holiday drink." His lips, those full, sexy lips I know to be punishing and wicked in all the right ways curve above his goatee. "Truce?"

"We're not fighting."

"You're angry with me."

"A truce doesn't shut down emotions, Savage."

He scowls a familiar, intense scowl. Everything he does is intense, which I used to love. What I don't love is his response. "Stop fucking calling me that."

75

"Stop cursing at me," I snap back.

"Make me."

"You might kill me if I try. I don't like my odds. I don't have a gun on me right now. I'm going for a run." His hands are full and I take a few steps, planning to pass him by, but that doesn't work.

Somehow he gets rid of the cups, and catches my arm, turning me to face him, heat radiating up my arm and over my chest. And then I'm staring into his eyes again, the past punching between us, the attraction, the connection still so damn alive that it steals my breath.

"You think that's all I am?" he challenges. "A killer?"

"I don't pretend to know who you are," I whisper, fighting the emotions balling in my chest again. "You left here a surgeon and came back ten years later an assassin."

"Eight years," he bites out. "And I wasn't an assassin. I was—something far more complex. Something that got out of hand. I work for good men now, doing good things."

"I need to take a run and get back."

"I'll go with you the way I used to."

"No," I say. "No, you *will not* go with me."

"Then I'll wait right here until you return."

"Stop touching me," I plead because I'm coming undone because I'm forgetting all the reasons he's bad and this, us, is trouble.

"I don't want to stop touching you. I've waited so damn long to touch you again. I didn't think I'd *ever* touch you again."

"You made that choice," I say, my voice lifting. "You. Not me."

"To protect you."

"And yet you're here now," I counter.

"Protecting you is no longer about staying away."

"That's it?" I demand. "You were protecting me by staying away? Really, Rick? Because while I cried myself to sleep over you, I didn't feel protected. I thought you were dead. And then that damn letter you wrote to me. You *destroyed* me. So forgive me if I don't feel *protected*." I jerk

76

at my arm. "Let go. Let go now or I swear I will start screaming."

His jaw clenches but he releases me, holding up his hands. "I'm sorry. I'm *so* sorry."

"It's not enough. It will *never* be enough. I'm engaged to another man."

"Do you love him?"

I feel the punch of that question but I recover quickly. I hold up my finger and the ring. "I'm wearing his ring."

"That's not an answer. Just tell me you love him. Tell me you love him and I'll go away."

"You don't get to give me an ultimatum. You don't have that right. Goodbye, *Savage*." I take off down the stairs and start running. I run hard and fast and I don't stop until I can't take a breath any longer. I tell myself not to turn around, but I do and he's not there. Rick didn't follow. It was that easy to get rid of him. Of course, it was. It was always easy to get rid of Rick Savage. I start running again, trying to beat down the pain spreading through my body and cutting at my heart.

When I finally reach my house again, I hate the blast of disappointment I feel when he's not here. I climb the stairs and freeze at the sight of a note shoved in the door. And damn it, my knees are weak as I grab it and open it to read: *See you tonight, beautiful.*

CHAPTER FOURTEEN

Candace

I arrive at the mansion in a pair of leggings at three o'clock, a good two hours before I was instructed by a commanding text message sent by Gabriel hours before, but I do so with good reason. I need a little work time in his office. I let myself into the mansion and the housekeeper, a fifty-something Hispanic woman named Bianca, just happens to be sweeping up near the door. "You're early," she greets, jabbing loose black hair back into the bun at the top of her head.

"Traffic is nuts," I say. "And I have a work call I was afraid would run over. This way I'm here and ready for the stylist when it's done."

"Very smart. None of the staff is here, of course, since it's Saturday, so you'll have the offices to yourself. Make yourself at home. It's almost your home anyway."

I smile, praying it doesn't look as wickedly stiff as it feels, before rushing upstairs and entering said extra office, which is attached to Gabriel's office. I dump my garment bag in a chair and then set my briefcase on the mahogany desk that sits in front of a wall of windows. Once I have my sketch pad out, I open my MacBook as well, just for show. I then grab my phone and click to the photo I'd taken from a phone I'd picked up from Gabriel's desk just before he proposed and now believe was some sort of burner phone. A way he communicates with someone to ensure the messages are not hacked or seen. Only I saw them.

The message exchange reads:

The general has to go sooner rather than later but after the wedding. I'm going to rush the proposal. That means you need to speed things up. He's becoming difficult. He needs to know that I can take everything from him, including her. If that doesn't work, we'll end him in a more final fashion.

Even before those messages, I'd sensed something was off with Gabriel. I'd been ready to break things off. He'd proposed only days later and I'd accepted to protect my father, who was gone then and is still gone now. I don't know what those messages mean, but nothing good, that's for sure. Finally, I have a chance to look for answers.

Heart beating a million miles an hour, I kick off my lace-free sneakers and rush to the connecting door that leads to Gabriel's lobby. Easing it open, I peek into the dark room. Once I'm sure the coast is clear, I step inside, shut the door again, and then rush to Gabriel's office. I try to open the door. The knob doesn't turn. "Damn it," I murmur. "No. No. No." But yes. Of course, it's locked. What the heck was I thinking?

I rush to his secretary's desk and open it, digging in a drawer and then another, until I find a key. Please let this be to his door. I hurry back to his office and try the lock. It doesn't fit. Breathing out in frustration, I do the only thing left to do. I sit down at his secretary's desk and start taking photos of random documents without even looking at what they are. I just shoot as many photos as I can. Fifteen minutes later, I have what must be hundreds of shots when voices sound just beyond the offices. *Gabriel's* voice. My heart lurches and I quickly shut the desk, but before I have time to escape, the lobby door begins to open. I dive under the desk, praying his secretary isn't the female voice I'm hearing.

The next thing I know there's a rush of movement, and the sound of two people doing what I believe to be kissing. "Holy hell, woman, I need to be inside you," Gabriel murmurs roughly.

"As your campaign manager," the female says. A female that I now know to be the gorgeous, twenty-something,

Monica Martin. "I do believe," she adds, "it's in your best interest to fuck away all your stress."

"Shouldn't I do that with my fiancée?" he asks.

"Why, when you'd rather be fucking me?" she challenges. "She's good for your presidency. I'm the one who'll keep you satisfied when she can't do the job."

I hold my breath, trying not to make a sound, fighting the tears that want to burn my eyes. I don't love him, but I've dated the man for a year. I've agreed to marry him and to be this used, to be this abused, hurts so damn badly.

"Fuck me," Monica demands. "Fuck me on your desk," she says, and thank God, I can hear them move in that direction. I can hear his door open and then shut. I poke my head out from under the desk, confirm I'm alone and then ease carefully out from under the desk. Once I'm on my feet, it's all I can do not to run, but I force myself to tiptoe forward and ease the door I'd come in open, slip inside the other room, and then seal the door.

Leaning against the door, I try to figure out how much danger I'm in by being here now. I can't be here, I decide. With a plan in my mind, I hurry to the desk, slide on my sneakers, load my briefcase, grab my purse, and head for the door. Slipping into the hallway, I quietly hurry past Gabriel's office area and down the stairs to make my way to the kitchen.

Bianca is standing behind the giant gray stone island of the magnificent chef's kitchen when I enter. "I'm starving," I announce. "Is there anything to eat by chance?"

Her eyes light predictably, as I've learned this past year that she loves to feed everyone. "You sit." She motions to a stool on the other side of the island. "I'll take care of you and your belly right away. You're too thin as it is."

I do as she orders, and soon, I have coffee and sugar cookies in front of me, which I force myself to nibble on, despite the churn of my stomach. I'm on cookie number three and coffee refill number two and Gabriel has yet to show himself. Apparently, he's still buried inside his campaign manager while plotting a way to bury my father.

CHAPTER FIFTEEN

Candace

"I'm going to just sit at the table and get some work done," I say, and Bianca quickly helps me settle next to the window. "Oh no," I say. "I left my sketchpad in the office."

"I'll grab it for you," Bianca offers and soon she's gone to grab it, and I'm alone.

I quickly draw a deep breath and try to calm my nerves, managing to bring myself down about five notches. I have to figure out how to get out of this. How to survive it. How to make sure my father survives it. I have to fight for him while he's off fighting for our country. I just pray nothing in those messages means he's not coming back. I press my hands to my face. God. Please no.

"You okay, honey?"

At Bianca's voice, I glance up. "Yes. Of course. A bit of a headache is all."

"I'll get you some medicine right now," she says, setting my sketchpad down on the table.

"Thank you," I say, and a few minutes later, fresh coffee, Advil, and another cookie later, I'm alone again, pretending to sketch because I know every common room in this place has cameras. Exactly why I can't bury my face in my hands again. That might give away how aware I am of a problem I'm not supposed to perceive. Still, I randomly check the photos I've taken at Gabriel's secretary's desk, but nothing jumps out at me as relevant to Gabriel's intent to hurt my father. And he *does* intend to hurt my father.

My phone buzzes with a text and I grab it to read: *I don't know how I'm going to watch that man touch you tonight and not kill him.*

I swallow hard and squeeze my eyes shut. I'm vulnerable right now and I know it. A part of me wants a hero to rescue me when I've learned I need to be my own heroine. He's a mercenary. He killed people for money. I don't love this man. I love the one I thought he once was. I reply with: *Because you're a killer?*

Because you belong with me.

Says the man who left me and never looked back. Pain rips through me, the kind of pain I should have felt when my fiancé was buried inside his campaign manager but did not. *Go away, Savage,* I reply.

I will never make that mistake again, is his reply. *And one day you'll call me Rick again.*

I scowl at my phone and punch a fast reply: *How about asshole? How about jerk? How about asshole?*

You already said asshole, he responds.

I grimace and type: *Bastard!*

You can be more creative, he challenges. *Why don't you meet me? Seeing my face might inspire new word choices. As a bonus, you can hit me a few times and I can kiss you again. You can even kiss me back if you want to. Even better, we can get naked and work out all of your anger. It might take a month but I'm good for it if you are.*

Are you done now? I challenge this time.

Never, he answers. *Not with you. That's the point.*

"The stylist is here early!" Bianca announces and this extra time to plan a way to deal with Gabriel is lost, at least, for now.

I'm whisked out of the kitchen and end up in one of the many spare bedrooms inside the mansion, this one with its own bathroom. The stylist, Karen, is a gorgeous black woman in her mid-thirties in a stylish pair of cream-colored pants she's paired with a cream-colored tank, and she presents me with a rack of stunning gowns with labels such as Valentino, Gucci, Chanel, and Fendi, and then leaves me alone for a few minutes to try them on.

84

I scan the dresses, aware that most girls might feel spoiled by the clothes, the private stylist, even the giant rock on my hand. Most girls who didn't just listen to their fiancé tell another woman how much he wanted to be inside her right after finding out he wants to ruin her father. I feel dirty. I feel trapped and my only escape is thinking about my text messages that haven't gone off again. Rick is silent. I hate how much I want him to text me again.

I barely look at the dresses that feel a part of the role I'm playing in a bad movie destined to deliver a bad ending. I latch onto a simple black knee-length Chanel dress with sheer long sleeves and a V-neck. Karen returns while I'm inspecting it in a full-length mirror. She offers me her critical eye. "It fits well, but anything would. You have a cute, petite figure, but it's a very simple choice," she assesses, crinkling her nose.

I slip out of it and into a robe. "It's Chanel and five thousand dollars," I counter. "It's not simple. Where do you want me for hair and make-up?"

She hangs the dress back on the rack, purses her lips and then points to the bathroom. Thankfully, we don't argue over the dress. She, in fact, turns on holiday music, singing along while she works on me. I, in turn, consider my desperate need to warn my father about all of this, but that's a near-impossible task. He's gone. He's overseas and any message I might send will likely be intercepted. Gabriel was CIA. He's still connected to the CIA. I could ask Rick for help, but I reject that idea. My father told me that he became a mercenary, a paid killer. That's not the man I knew. I can't trust him. I did that once and it destroyed me. And besides, he's here now, but for all I know, he'll be gone tomorrow. He's also got military connections. One word spoken to the wrong person and my father might suffer. *I can't go to him.* In fact, the way I see it, if Rick makes Gabriel feel threatened, Gabriel may act against my father sooner than later. He's already on the sooner than later path, per that text message I copied.

I'm back to Rick Savage needing to go away. If he sends me another text message, I won't reply. If he shows up

CHAPTER SIXTEEN

Candace

Forty-five minutes later, I'm in the black Chanel dress, and thanks to the talented stylist, my brown hair is a mahogany silk that I could never recreate at home, flowing around my shoulders. My makeup is elegant roses and pinks with the exception of my lips, which are painted a bold red because, per Karen, I need accents to pop with such a simple dress. Following her lead, I choose a pair of red velvet pumps and a matching hip purse, telling myself it's inspired by my makeup. My choice has nothing to do with Rick's promise that he'll see me tonight or his love of me in red. It certainly has nothing to do with the way the color red inspired the nickname "Candy." I just need that pop. Karen said so. And there's no way Rick will be at this event anyway. Security will be tight. He'll be shut out. I wish I could say the same of myself.

"You look lovely," Karen says. "Absolutely lovely." She eyes her watch. "You had better head downstairs. I understand your car is picking you up right about now."

I puff out a breath with the realization that I now have to pretend to be okay with Gabriel. I have to smile. I have to touch him and let him touch me.

"Thank you, Karen," I say, practicing my smile because she deserves it. "You're gifted and I appreciate you making me a recipient of those gifts."

"If it's true, and he runs for president and wins, you will be the most beautiful first lady of all."

"You are too kind," I say, my throat thick, my mouth cotton. "Thank you, again."

"Is it true?" she nudges. "Is he running?"

"I don't know that answer," I say. "I don't think he does either. Not yet." *But,* I add silently, *if I have my way, he will never run this country.*

We laugh about this or that and too soon, I'm heading down the stairs to find Gabriel waiting below and dressed in a tuxedo. He is as handsome as ever, handsomely evil. Because that's what he is. Evil. I will never see him any other way again, and for a moment, I think of Rick, of staring into his eyes this morning. He's a confessed mercenary, a hired killer, and yet that's not what I see when I'm with him. That's not what I feel when I'm with him. I don't know what that means. Love is blind? And I still love him?

All I know is that thinking about Rick right now is what gets me down the stairs without falling down. The idea that I might see him tonight is what keeps me steady when it should unsteady me.

"You look lovely," Gabriel says as I join him, his gaze sliding up and down my body. His voice lowering as he adds, "I'll show you how lovely when we're alone."

Because apparently, one woman in a day isn't enough for him. "Thank you," I say tightly.

His gaze narrows sharply. "Something wrong?"

"Just a little nervous," I assure him, reprimanding myself for being too transparent. "It's my first event on your arm as your fiancée."

He strokes my hair and it's all I can do not to shrink away from the touch. "You'll be perfect tonight. You always are." He offers me his arm.

Without a real option, I settle my hand in the crook of his elbow, and a few minutes later we're in the back of a town car, his palm under my dress, high on my thigh. I want to hit him, but instead, my hand settles delicately on top of his hand and, desperate to offset my behavior, I dare to kiss his cheek. It's a mistake. He cups my head and comes in for a deep kiss. My tongue is now in the same mouth that Monica's tongue was in only hours before if it's been that long. Finally, he pulls back and I just want out of this car.

Part of me wishes I wasn't wearing stay-on lipstick. Then maybe he'd keep his mouth off of me.

Thankfully, his cellphone rings and he takes the call that lasts until we arrive at the hotel hosting the event. Gabriel ends his call not a second before the valet is opening his door. "The show has begun," he says, glancing over at me. "Ready?"

"Yes," I say, but he's barely even noticed my reply. He's already sliding out of the car.

With an intake of breath, I scoot along after him. He does offer me his hand, of course, because cameras flash. He inches me up close to him and whisks me in the door, a high ceiling with a dangling chandelier above our heads. It's here in the lobby, with clusters of fine furnishings and art around us, that we're greeted by random familiar faces. My fake smile all but breaks my face, but it stays in place. Finally, we're in a great room with a small orchestra at the front, clusters of white covered tables, and an early Christmas tree in the corner. But none of that is what I'm looking at or for. It's him, it's Rick. I'm apparently obsessed with the idea of him being here, my gaze whipping through the crowd, cutting left and right, seeking him out before he seeks us out. And he might. Lord help me, what is he going to do if he does show up?

"What do you see?" Gabriel asks, sounding a bit suspicious.

I grin. "Our next stop," I say, pointing to a chocolate fountain, knowing full well Gabriel will not be caught stuffing his face. "I haven't eaten much today."

"You and your chocolate," he comments, his posture softening, whatever edge I'd created in him with my behavior softening into a low laugh.

"Only sometimes," I say, trying to sound as if I'm teasing. Which I am, because I prefer chocolate over him, every moment of every day.

Monica is suddenly standing in front of us, looking oh so Marilyn Monroe, her pink dress hugging all her many curves, the way she was hugging my fiancé a few hours ago. Her blonde hair is even an extra shade of bleached right now. "You look stunning, Candace," she proclaims. "A future first lady for sure."

"As do you," I say and, unable to stop myself from taking a tiny jab, I add, "A future first lady, for sure." It infers I know she's fucking Gabriel yes, but it's tamer than me telling her she looks like the White House bimbo.

Her eyes go wide. "What?" She glances at Gabriel and then me. "A first—lady?"

"I just meant that you're stunning," I assure her, glancing at Gabriel. "Isn't she, honey?"

He studies me under half-veiled lashes. "She is," he agrees, his hand sliding to my lower back, leaning in close to whisper in my ear, "But not the way you are."

And yet, he's fucking her, I think, but I manage to smile up at him and say, "Chocolate. I must indulge. Touch base with Monica. You know where to find me." I kiss his cheek and hurry away. Some may say the very fact that I'm willing to leave him with the woman he was just buried inside is a testament to how much I never loved him. Or perhaps how much I love another man, who is also somewhere in this room.

I weave through the quickly thickening crowd, greeted by a person here or there, suffocating from the fakeness. Cutting right, I stop at the chocolate fountain and dip a marshmallow into the drip, my skin tingling with awareness. The kind of awareness I've only ever felt with one man. The kind of awareness I'd convinced myself was nothing more than a Cinderella memory, a fantasy I'd created in my mind. I can barely breathe. My nipples pucker. My sex clenches. I eat the damn marshmallow and tell myself to focus on it. *He's* not here. He can't get past security and just because he says he'll be here means nothing. He said he'd be back, too, and well I guess technically, that wasn't a lie. He came back. *Ten years too late.*

I'm just licking chocolate off my finger in a very "me" fashion that Gabriel would not likely appreciate when my phone buzzes with a text message. It's from *him*. I know it's from him, and I'm not sure if I want him to tell me that's he's not coming or that he's already here. I reach in my purse, pull out my cell and read a message from Rick: *I'm not sure which one of us enjoyed you eating that marshmallow more, you or me?*

My gaze jerks up with the suggestive message that confirms Rick isn't just here. He's close.

CHAPTER SEVENTEEN

Candace

Reeling from Rick's text message, my heart racing, I scan the crowd looking for his location, certain he's right here, close, so very close. Too close. Not close enough. This man has me twisted in confusing knots. My phone beeps with another message, but before I can read it, a sixty-something-year-old woman joins me by the chocolate fountain, demanding my attention. "You know how to enjoy your chocolate. I love you already." Her hands sparkle with jewels, her dress glistening with sequins. "I'm Nicole Cook," she continues. "Judge Nicole Cook. A happy donor to Gabriel's campaign."

She wants to talk about Gabriel. I want to read that message and find Rick. But I do what survival for me and my father demands I do right now. I focus on Gabriel's life, promising myself that it won't be mine soon. "So nice to meet you," I manage, glancing over the judge's shoulder and expecting Rick to be there. He's not, but my skin prickles with awareness. Maybe he's behind me. Maybe he's right there about to touch me. The judge says something I don't catch. I will myself to focus on this new conversation that's now holding me prisoner, much like Gabriel has now kidnapped my life. Actually, I'm not sure Rick hasn't as well. The men in my life, past and present, seem to have far more control than I think I realized until this moment.

"That chocolate's tempting me as well," she teases. "I might just have to scoop it up with my finger any minute now."

My cheeks burn red. "Please don't hold my finger-licking chocolate habits against him."

"Quite the contrary," she assures me. "You're as real as they come. To me, that says he is as well."

And there it is. The reason he fucks Monica and drapes me over his arm. I'm real and I help to validate the stupid "Honest Gabe" slogan. So does my father, though apparently, Honest Gabe is about to take him down. Until now, I thought that meant destroying his career, but when I consider how that affects his campaign, I don't see how it would justify such an action.

Nicole begins rambling on about Gabriel and how wonderful he is, but the idea that I'm around because I'm good for his reputation has me thinking about Monica's comment earlier. She said I was the one who belonged on his arm. Gabriel's reputation is everything to him. How is he going to deal with my father without damaging himself? There's only one answer. He's going to kill him. It's ridiculous. It's insane. Of course, he's not going to kill him. Or rather, have him killed. He's not going to do that. Suddenly, I'm feeling more than a little claustrophobic.

I'm about to make an excuse to escape when Gabriel joins us, and the instant his hand touches my back, I'm fighting that recoil reaction all over again. How am I going to have sex with this man again? How? I can't and that means starting the sick routine now. I grab his arm and push to my toes to whisper, "I'm not feeling well. I'm going to find a bathroom."

He inches backward and studies my face. "That's not good."

"I'll try not to breathe on you." I smile at Nicole. "Nice to meet you. I'll see you soon." With that, I fade into the crowd and while I could find a spot to avoid Rick and Gabriel, I'm about to explode with all of this avoidance. I'm sick of avoidance. I'm ready to fight. I'm not sure what that means just yet, but I'm going to figure it out, starting now. I can't confront Gabriel until I figure out this thing with my father, but I damn sure can confront Rick. This first battle will be step one of me reclaiming the control I've somehow allowed to be swiped right out of my hands and heart. This thought has me fuming. How did I let myself get sucked into Gabriel's plan to rule the world? The answer comes easily: Rick. Rick wouldn't let go of me and I was desperate to escape his hold. This is all his fault, which actually isn't true. I'm responsible for me and my actions, but he still deserves my anger.

I head toward the back of the room, my skin tingling with the certainty that's he's watching me, that he's pursuing me, and that I've invited it. What's scary is the thrill that shoots through me, the heat burning low in my belly, just knowing that I'm about to be with him again. To talk, I remind myself. This is all about talking.

I cut left, and walk down a hallway, then up a set of stairs that I know from several other events I've attended at the venue leads to the upper level and a private balcony. That's how all in I am on this talk with Savage. I'm leading us to privacy.

Once I'm on the second level, I could cut to the right to overlook the party from the railing, but instead, I turn left again. A quick walk down a winding hallway ends at a set of wood-trimmed double glass doors, which are presently standing open, in evident invitation onto an outdoor terrace. I exit into the night air, a hint of November in the chill of the wind. In front of me and winding left and right is a thick white balcony overlooking the popular River Walk. Clusters of two seated tables with candles on top sit between me and that railing.

Nerves erupt inside me and I step around the open door, head behind it, and lean on the wall where I wait on Rick. I just want to look at him the way he was just looking at me, to assess his motives, to decide what he's after. I just want the luxury of watching the man I almost called my husband, without questions or demands. I just need a moment or ten to feel like I'm in control.

I squeeze my eyes shut because this very need proves that I'm not in control. I'm not even close to in control. I'm a woman engaged to a man I'd rather stab in the leg with a pencil than kiss, and yet kiss him I must.

The air shifts and goosebumps leap across my skin. I open my eyes to find Rick standing there right in front of me, towering over me. At six foot five inches to my mere five foot four inches, he's always been overwhelmingly large. And I like it. I *liked* it, I amend quickly.

And his cologne, it's still that woodsy wonderful scent that's as familiar as his intense stare and solid jawline. And Lord help me, this man is a barbarian of brutal perfection in a tuxedo.

"You, Candace," he says softly, "you are more breathtaking than I remember, and just to be clear, I remembered you as more breathtaking than the only star in a pitch dark warzone-driven night."

His voice doesn't lift, but he says those words like they are ripped straight from his soul. They certainly rip right through my heart. I am warm and cold in the same moment, tormented with need for this man, who will just hurt me again. And I won't survive falling for him and losing him again.

"Stop," I whisper. "Stop doing what you're doing." My voice trembles with emotion I want to call hate, but this isn't hate. Hate would be easy and nothing with Rick Savage is easy, not any more.

"All I'm doing is speaking from my heart," he professes.

He's hit about ten nerves with that statement. "Your heart?" I demand, my reaction fierce and fast. "*Your heart?!*" I step into him and punch his chest. "Your heart? What about *my* heart?" I punch him again.

He catches my wrist and I hate the sizzle that shoots through my body. I hate the way his big hands make me feel small and vulnerable and yet so damn perfectly female. "I hope like hell I still have your heart," he murmurs. "Because you have mine, baby. You have it. You have *always* had it."

"Me and how many hundreds of other women?"

"No one but you."

"And yet you left and stayed away? I don't need lies. I'm sick of lies. Stop playing me. Just say it. What do you want? Why are you here?"

He pulls me closer and then backs me up again, pressing me against the wall, his powerful thighs caging mine. "I shouldn't have left. I shouldn't have stayed away. Things happened and I didn't want to pull you down with me. I didn't feel worthy."

"Then what does that make me? Unworthy right along with you? Right. *That's* what it makes me."

"No. Fuck. No." He releases my hands and presses his to the wall on either side of me. "You—"

"I wasn't enough for you and it doesn't matter. Not anymore." I shove my ring between us. "I'm engaged to another man."

He catches my hand. "If you shove that *fucking* ring at me one more time, I will take it off your finger and shove it up his puckered, lying politician ass."

"You don't have that right."

"Oh I do, baby. I do have a right. You're mine. Not his."

"I am not yours. I stopped being yours when you sent me that letter. No. No, the truth is, I stopped being yours the day you deployed. The letter is just when I finally got let in on our story. The one that ended, *Savage*. We ended and you have no—"

I never finish that statement. His hand comes down on the back of my head, his tongue stroking past my teeth, and it's too much. Too much him. Too much temptation. Too much to fight. I can't breathe without him. I've never been able to breathe without him. I moan with the wicked rasp of his tongue against mine, the taste of him—wild, wicked man—everything I want and miss, even need. I burn right here in my shoes, burn right here in his arms. I sink into the kiss, and for just a few moments, I pretend that he never left, that he won't leave again. I let myself just go home and he is my home. He has always been my home and I have been forever lost since he left.

"You belong to me," he murmurs against my lips.

Panic overtakes me. I can't blow this with Gabriel. My father's life might depend on it. I push against the man I want and hate and love. I push hard and he holds on the way he never did before. The way he won't in the future. "That kiss meant nothing," I hiss, anger and emotions blasting through me.

"Do you love him?"

"You don't even have the right to ask me that question."

"No is the answer," he says. "No, you *do not* love him. You can barely stand for that man to touch you. I watched you with him. I saw how you are with that bastard. And I know you, Candy. I know that there's something going on. What are you afraid of?"

"Don't call me Candy. And what am I afraid of? *You*. I'm afraid of you."

His hands slide under my hair to my neck. "I fucked up, baby. I fucked us up, but I'm here now."

"Until you leave again?"

"Never again. Ever. And if you run, I will follow you to the other side of the world if I have to catch you to love you. Whatever is going on right now, you are not alone."

"I don't even know you anymore."

"You know me. You know me like no one else knows me."

He cups my face, tilting my gaze to his. "I haven't been the hero you deserve, but I'm here now. I will be now, but you have to tell me what kind of trouble you're in."

I want to. I want to trust him. I want him to be the man I used to know and love. But he left and my father warned me that Rick Savage was trouble, a hired killer to avoid. "Because you declare everything is different now, I'm supposed to trust you?" I ask, and I realize too late that that question isn't a denial of a problem. It's me denying him my trust.

He proves that understanding by vowing, "I'm going to make you trust me."

"The way you made me fall for you?"

Muffled voices sound in the near distance, rapidly growing closer, my spine stiffening. "I have to go back down." I grab his lapel. "There are things in my life you can't understand. One of them is why I have to go downstairs."

"Because you're in trouble?"

"Yes. Because trouble is standing right in front of me."

"Trouble from everyone but you, baby." His lips press into a tight line. "Go back down. I'll come to you tonight."

"You'll come to me tonight? You can't—"

"I am. I will."

"I'll be with *him*."

"No," he says with absoluteness. "You *will not* be with him. He's going to be otherwise occupied."

I blink. "What does that even mean?"

"Candace!"

At Gabriel's voice, my eyes go wide, my heart lurching. I grab Rick's arm. My father and Gabriel and—just—"I can't be seen with you. I beg of you—"

He cups my head and kisses me. "I told you not to beg. Ever. Don't kiss him or I swear to you, I'll kill him." He releases me and cuts to the right, disappearing into the shadows and around a corner. I force myself to move, to push off the wall and I'm just about to re-enter the hotel when Gabriel steps in front of me.

CHAPTER EIGHTEEN

Candace

Gabriel's eyes rake over my face and then drop to my cleavage. "You look good enough to eat," he murmurs, and before I know his intent, he's manhandled me into a back step. Suddenly, I'm against the same wall I was against minutes before with Rick, but this time it's Gabriel who presses against me. My reaction this time isn't heat and desire, mixed with a need to protect myself from a broken heart. I want him off of me.

"Stop," I say, shoving against him. "Stop." He leans in to kiss me and oh God, Rick said don't let him kiss me. And I don't want him to kiss me. I turn my head. "I don't feel well."

"I'll make you feel better." His hand cups my backside and squeezes. The air charges and that's exactly what I expect Rick to do: charge. Desperation fills me and I lift a knee that lands in his groin. He grunts and doubles over. "What the fuck, Candace?" he growls, holding his groin and glaring at me. "What the fuck?"

"I'm sick. I *told you* that."

He straightens and scowls. "So you kneed me? Really, Candace?"

"Would you rather me have thrown up on you? And trying to feel me up at a charity event isn't any more presidential than when you—" I stop myself before I say "fucked your campaign manager."

"Than when I what?" he snaps.

"Cursed at me," I say quickly. "I'm sick. I needed air and you were groping me like a teenager, not a future president.

Unless you plan to be one of the ones who settles between every woman's legs like it's your right."

"What? Why would you even say that? You're sick and talking crazy. Holy hell. You're not pregnant, are you? Because if you are—"

"I'm sick and you attacked me, which means I'm crazy and pregnant? Are you really serious right now?"

"I didn't attack you."

"Who are you right now?" I demand. "And for the record, I'm not pregnant. I'm on birth control."

"There's still a chance. You need to take a test."

"So glad you're worried about me," I snap, crossing my arms in front of me. If Rick didn't already know something was up with me and Gabriel, he knows now. "Of course, though. I'll take the test. To put your mind at ease."

"Holy hell," Gabriel murmurs and then steps in front of me, his hands coming down on my arms, his touch having now become darn near revolting. "A baby is a good thing."

Spoken in front of Rick Savage. The man has no idea how hard he's trying to end up dead. Or how much I need to speak to the other man in the vicinity right now. And I do with my response. "We aren't married, Gabriel," I say, "and I'm not ready for kids," I remind him.

"I'm just telling you that I wouldn't be unhappy. We'd just have to rush the wedding."

And there it is. The reason he's all about me being pregnant. He needs to control my father, and he feels like I need to be locked down before he acts against him. Bastard.

"I'm sorry, buttercup," he adds.

Buttercup.

I thought that was an endearment. Now I see it as a pet's name. That's what I am: his pet.

Candy is different.

It's about pleasure. It's about Rick finding me sexy, making me *feel* sexy. My God, I'm comparing my fiancé to my ex-fiancé, but why is this new? I've compared every man to Rick.

"The pressure is wearing on me," Gabriel continues. "I took it out on you. I'll make it up to you tonight."

God, I hope not. I hope Rick really has a plan to get rid of him that doesn't include killing him, of course. Rick being a hired killer is hard to get my head around.

"Don't you have a speech to give?" I ask, trying to end this encounter with Gabriel before it becomes an encounter with Rick and Gabriel at the same time. "We need to get back downstairs."

"Right." He glances at his watch. "We need to get back down there. Are you coming? I'd like to have you by my side. I'm always better with you by my side."

A statement he makes often. It used to please me, but now I know that it's just another way to call me his pet. "I'm okay right now. Let's go before that changes or someone thinks we're up to no good."

He gives a wicked laugh and starts walking, dragging his fake sick fiancée with him. And I am fake sick. I'm also his fake fiancée. Rick knows. He knows and he's going to want answers. And I have until I leave this party to decide if I'm going to trust him. The problem is that I'm not sure what I decide here and now matters. That man vowed to make me fall for him and I did. He's my kryptonite. If he wants to make me trust him, he'll come at me like the bull he is, and he won't stop coming until he has what he wants. And I'm not sure yet what that is. Maybe it's me, but even if it is, for how long?

Savage

I grab the balcony and hold tight, because that's the only way I'm going to stop myself from beating Gabriel's ass, right here, right now, in this hotel. I imagine my hands on his neck. I imagine the many ways I could kill him and how much better this world would be without him. I wouldn't regret getting rid of him, but I already know that's going to be a problem for Candace. She's got morals. I lost mine the day I left her behind.

Adam steps to my side, grabbing hold of the railing. "There you go proving me right," he says. "I heard it all and I wanted to kill that bastard. I really wanted to kill him and I don't even know Candace. You, you love her."

"I let him walk because I can't kill him here and now and win her back. I did, however, fantasize about ten ways to do it later." I glance over at him. "Still think he's a good guy?"

"No. No, I don't. I think I just got an insider's view of how he'd run the country. That's not, however, a reason to kill him."

"Give him time. He'll think one up for you." I turn on my elbow to face Adam and he does the same. "That fucker has something on her, which probably translates to her father."

"You mean to Tag's operation?"

"Tag pulling me into this says yes." My lips press together. "But I should have been here a long fucking time ago." A muscle in my jaw ticks. "I owe him a painless death for bringing me back. I need to get Candace alone, away from here. Tell me we arranged his departure tonight because I will kill him before he touches her again."

"We did. And we have back-up. Asher just got in tonight."

I scowl. I do a lot of scowling around Adam the fucking SEAL Team Six boy scout. "I say stay out of this and Walker dives in deeper. What dweeb made that call?"

He straightens uncomfortably in a tuxedo too small for him, a disadvantage for his agility should I decide to beat his ass. "You're the dweeb if you think that you can protect her and take on Tag without help. Asher was Team Six with me."

"How many times do I have to hear SEAL Team Six?"

"I trust him," he says. "And he's a hacker. Not as great as Blake, but he's good. We need him."

"What I need is off this balcony." I turn away from him and start walking. By the time I'm in the hallway, he's by my side. Bastard thinks I'm going to lose my shit and kill Gabriel. He might be right.

"You don't have anything else to say about Asher showing up?" he asks.

I smirk. "You can't fix stupid and apparently, SEALs are stupid."

"Bastard," he says.

"Boy scout," I snap.

"Scrooge."

"Bastard."

We've made it almost to the roundabout when Candace is suddenly in front of me and to my shock, her hands go to my chest. I have about two seconds to revel in her willingness to touch me before she says, "Your dad's here." I feel those words like a knife plunging into my chest. "I didn't know," she continues. "I would have warned you. I haven't seen him in years. I don't know why he's here."

I don't outwardly react, but it's equivalent to a donkey kicking and squealing inside my brain right now. "Where?"

"He's at a table near the stage." She glances awkwardly at Adam.

"Adam," Adam says. "I'm a friend."

"A stupid as fuck ex-Navy SEAL on SEAL Team Six or some shit like that," I say. "But a friend."

"Oh," she says, her eyes go wide and flick to Adam. "Thank you for your service," she says.

"You didn't thank me for my service," I point out.

She pulls her hands away from my chest and folds her arms in front of her. A cold spot burns in my chest where she'd touched me and it burns hollow. "Thank you for your service, Rick," she says.

"That sounded more like: fuck you, I hate you, Rick Savage."

"I don't hate," she says, dropping her hands, "and I do very much respect your service." She lowers her voice. "Have you seen him? Your father?"

"No, and I couldn't give a shit about that man. *You* are another story. I'm about thirty seconds from throwing you over my shoulder and carrying you out of here. I thought I should warn you."

"Right. I need to get back downstairs before I'm missed." She turns and I suddenly realize what's going on here. My father was a big part of why I left. She's afraid he's why I'll leave again. She doesn't want me to leave. Thank fuck for that.

I step forward and catch her arm, lowering my voice for her ears only. "I'm not going anywhere without you, baby."

She scrapes her teeth over her lip and whispers, "We'll see." She pulls away from me and then she's gone.

Adam steps to my side. "What do I need to know right now?"

"My father's a dick. Avoid him. I do." I start walking and instead of heading down the stairs, I walk another path that leads me to the railing that overlooks the party. Adam doesn't immediately follow.

And so, I stand there alone, as I have most of this night, and scan the crowd, seeking the most important person in the room, the only person who matters in this room to me now or ever: Candace. She's near the stage where the orchestra is playing, talking with Gabriel and a group of three men. Next, I find my father mid-room, talking to a much younger woman. He looks old, his thick hair solid gray, his frame on the thin side, despite his love of the bottle. Maybe that's changed, but I doubt it.

I watch him, reaching deep for my emotional response, which is still hate. I hate that man. A security guard approaches him and my father looks flustered before leaving. Adam steps to my side. "Someone slashed his tires. Not really, but he won't know that until he's already in the parking lot."

I cast him an amused look. "I might just give you a cookie for that one."

"I'll take a new bottle of Johnnie Walker. Blue label. Expensive as fuck, but considering the death wish jobs you took when you started at Walker, you can afford it. And that's my drink."

I tune him out as Gabriel steps onto the stage and greets the crowd. Thank you, Lord, he doesn't take Candace with him. She's at the side of the stage, and her gaze scans the audience and then lifts to find me. Our eyes lock and hold. She doesn't look away. I'm so fucking stupid for walking away from her. I told her not to beg anyone for anything, but I'll beg for another chance. On my fucking knees. I will so fucking beg.

An older woman steps to her side and murmurs in her ear, the very action demanding her attention, as does Gabriel on the stage. He begins to speak, blowing smoke up the audience's asses with bullshit political promises. He also shouts, "Don't mess with Texas!" four freaking times.

I eye Adam, lift my jacket and motion to my gun, which I moved through security far too easily. "Shoot me. Just do it. Put me out of my fucked-up misery."

"Tempting," he says. "But no. You earned this torture by losing a woman that damn perfect."

She is perfect, and I pretty much want to poke his eyes out just for noticing, but I also want to share that Johnnie Walker with him, so I don't. Sooner than later, considering Gabriel is jabbering like a teenage boy who just saw his first set of nipples. Finally, he wraps things the fuck up.

Adam's phone buzzes and he checks his message. "Now," he says, lifting his chin toward the stage as a man rushes to Gabriel's side and whispers in his ear. A good ten people in the room receive text messages at the same time and scramble to read them. All of which will instruct them to immediately travel to Austin for a meeting with the governor. It's all planned, a crisis manufactured by Blake Walker's expert hacking skills.

Gabriel departs the stage and walks to Candace's side. He leans in too damn close to her, his fucking hand on her waist and murmurs close to her ear. There's a short exchange and he departs, leaving her behind. Her eyes cut through the crowd and lift to mine again. She knows now. He's leaving. I'm not.

CHAPTER NINETEEN

Candace

I slide into the backseat of the town car set to take me to Gabriel's mansion to grab my car and do so with only one thing on my mind: Rick. That look on his face when I told him his father was at the event. He's supposed to be a killer, a hired killer, cold and hard, and yet one mention of his father and he froze. He was relieved that I saved him that confrontation.

My fingers press to my lips, remembering the brutally wonderful touch of his mouth to mine. That kiss. His touch. His woodsy wonderful smell. The sea of torment that's always been there in the depths of those blue eyes even before I'd warned him about his father. I have always felt like he would drown in that torment, but I'd always sworn I'd go down with him. But he didn't let me. He left. He left and he never came back. And he'll leave again.

The car pulls to the front of the mansion, and I direct the driver to my spot under a willow tree. Just that quickly, I'm outside, nerves blasting my belly before I climb into my car. My empty car. Rick isn't here. I'm not sure why I believed he would be. Of course, he wouldn't have had time to make it here. Maybe I'm wrong. Maybe he won't come at all. His father has a way of driving him away. Maybe his father was all it took to repeat history.

Once I'm on the road, I mentally have a self-preservation conversation with myself.

He's not the man for me.

He's not the man I loved.

He's the man who will hurt me.

Again.

I knew that about him that first night we met at the coffee bar. I know that about him now. That's who he is. He's pain and torment. Those things live inside him and they bleed into his life. They bled into mine and when he left, I never stopped bleeding.

Turning onto my street, *our* street when he lived with me, I am one big adrenaline rush of anticipation. Approaching the house, I find no other cars. He's not here. The realization guts me. Proof that I'm a fool asking to be hurt again. God. He's not here. Maybe his father really did drive him away. Maybe he had to go to Austin like Gabriel. Maybe he won't be here until later. Maybe he won't be here at all. Maybe he's here for a job that demanded his attention and so, we're cut short. *Again.* It hurts already. He hurt me again already and all of this is made up in my head.

And I'm rambling in my own head. I'm losing it. I'm crazy over this man in every possible way.

I barely remember pulling into the garage and parking. I barely remember letting the door slide into place. I climb out of the car and lean against it. My mind flashing back to that first night here and the crash of my coffee on the ground. The passion in our kisses. The hunger in our touches. And then my father and Rick together in my kitchen. It felt like the beginning of forever. It was nothing more than a chapter. Fighting tears I swore I'd stop shedding for Rick Savage, I walk to the door and use my key to open it, When I step inside I shut it behind me and gasp.

He's here.

Rick is standing right in front of me, bigger than life, and so damn him, in that him kind of way that I couldn't explain if I tried. He steps closer and I drop my bag on the counter. He will hurt me again, I remind myself, but like that first night, I don't seem to care.

I step toward him, but he's already there, already here, right here with me. I can't even believe it's true. He folds me close, his big, hard body absorbing mine. His fingers tangle in my hair, his lips slanting over my lips. And then he's kissing me, kissing me with the intensity of a man who can't breathe without me. And I can't breathe without him. I haven't drawn a real breath since he sent me that letter.

My arms slide under his tuxedo jacket, wrapping his body, muscles flexing under my touch. The heat of his body burning into mine, sunshine warming the ice in my heart he created when he left. And that's what scares me. Just this quickly, I'm consumed by him, the princess and the warrior, as he used to call us. My man. My hero. And those are dangerous things for me to feel, so very dangerous. Because they're not real. He showed me that they aren't real.

"This means nothing," I say, tearing my mouth from his, my hand planting on the hard wall of his chest. "This is sex. Just sex. This changes nothing."

"Baby, we were never just sex."

"We are not the us of the past," I say, grabbing his lapel. "I just need—you owe me this. You owe me a proper—"

"Everything," he says. "In ways you don't understand, but, baby, you will. I promise you, you will."

I don't try to understand that statement and I really don't get the chance. His mouth is back on my mouth.

The very idea of forever with this man is one part perfect, another part absolute pain. Because there is no forever with this man. But he doesn't give me time to object to a fantasy I'll never own, that I'm not sure I want to try and own again. I don't need forever. I need right now. I need him. I sink back into the kiss and he's ravenous. Claiming me. Taking me. Kissing the hell out of me and God, I love it. God, I need it. I need *him*.

I reach for his tie and my hand, my damn ring, snags on his jawline. His mouth rips from mine, and he catches my hand, holding that ring between us. "If I ever see you in this ring again, I swear I will kill him."

"Are you trying to remind me that you're a killer?"

"I am a killer, Candace. I'm not going to deny who or what I am. But I saved lives, too. I saved good lives that needed to be saved. He's not one of those good lives. Decide now. Do I kiss you again or do I not? Because I'm not kissing you with that fucking ring on your hand. Take the ring off."

He lowers his voice. "Unless you keep calling me a killer because you're afraid of me."

Afraid of him.

He called himself unworthy. He really believes that.

I stare up at him, I search his face, and that's what I find there. Fear. Not mine, but his. He fears that I'm afraid of him, that he's not good enough for me because of what he's done, what he believes he's become. That's why he didn't come home. That's why he'll leave again, but I'm back to not caring. Not right now.

I don't want him to leave. I don't want him to stop kissing me. "There is no part of me that is afraid of you, Rick Savage." I pull the ring off my finger.

CHAPTER TWENTY

Savage

I throw that fucking ring as far as I can throw it and I wait for her to panic, but she doesn't. She pushes to her toes and leans into me, offering me what I want: her. My hand comes down on the back of her head and then I'm kissing the hell out of her, drinking her in, and this is not a gentle kiss. This is a rough, demanding, take-what-I-want kiss. She says she's not afraid of me. I want her to show me she's not afraid of me. I need her to show me she's all in. It doesn't matter that I have no right to make such a demand. It doesn't matter that I don't deserve this woman. Not tonight. Tonight, she's mine and I'm not settling for less than everything.

I mold her closer, my hands sliding up her back and I rotate her, pressing her against the wall, fingers walking her dress up her thighs until thank you, Jesus, I have that sweet little ass of hers in one of my hands. My other strokes her hair from her face, forcing her gaze to mine. "What color are your panties?"

"They're not red."

"Then you didn't expect me tonight."

"I haven't expected you in a very long time," she whispers.

"Now you know to wear red."

"Stop talking," she says, grabbing my tie and trying to yank it free. It doesn't budge and I pretend to choke.

"Oh God." She laughs. "That went better in my head."

Just that easily, the mood between us lightens, becoming this familiar push and pull of laughter and passion. "A for the effort, baby." I rip my tie away and cup her head, kissing her. "Killed by a bow tie. Appropriate considering how much I hate these monkey suits, don't you think?"

"I love you in a tuxedo."

Love. That's not a word she's chosen accidentally, and I want to hear it again. "Do you?"

"Yes," she breathes out softly. "*Very* much."

There is so much more than a compliment in those words. There are a million moments shared between us just like this one. Emotions pulse between us. "I'll take anything that isn't hate that I can get from you."

Her hand settles on my face, over my scar. "I told you, Rick Savage, I don't hate you." Her lashes lower and lift. "Okay, sometimes. Sometimes, I hate you."

And I deserve that hate. It stabs me, cuts me, burns right through me. I deserve it, but I reject it here, now, and in the future. I scoop her up and start walking, with one destination in mind: the bedroom. Our bedroom where we've shared passion, laughter, and so fucking much more. Candace curls into me, buries her face in my shoulder, seeking shelter with me, not from me. Her actions tell me there's hope. They also tell me it's not certain. Not yet.

I walk us up the stairs and into the bedroom. The bathroom light is on and I don't bother with another. I set her down at the foot of the bed, her back to my front, my hand settling on her belly. I lean in, folding her against me, inhaling that sweet floral scent that is so damn her, my lips at her ear. "I missed you so fucking much."

She twists around to face me. "Don't talk. Don't say things like that because then I start thinking. I think things like: then why the hell did you stay away?"

I pull her to me, catch her hair in my fingers and turn her gaze to mine. "Then fuck the hate out, baby, because I'm not going to hold back."

"I don't want you to right now, Rick."

"What do you want, baby?"

"You know what I want. What I've always wanted. *You.* Can I just pretend—"

"No. No, you cannot pretend. I need real from you, Candy, baby. I need real. If you hate me, show me. If you love me, show me." I turn her back around, my mouth by her ear again, my fingers dragging her dress down. "If you want me, *show me.*" My hands slide under the dress to settle on her bare shoulders. "And I'll show you." I slide the dress off her shoulders, and before it's even on the ground, her bra is unhooked and it's on the floor.

I cup her breasts and lean into her. She reaches for my face, reaches for my mouth, and then we're kissing, lips burning into lips.

She twists around to face me again and I've already molded her to me. "You are not his."

"You can't just come back and suddenly I'm yours."

"Just say—"

"I want you. I missed you. I just don't trust you not to leave again."

"I'm not going anywhere."

"I don't believe you."

"Fuck," I murmur, and I'm angry. So fucking angry. And not at her. At me. I kiss her hard and fast and turn her to the bed. I press her forward onto her hands, her beautiful backside in the air, and I grab the slip of black lace she's wearing and rip it away.

She gasps and I smack her backside. She arches forward and I lean forward, my body caging her body, and I show her the panties. "You wore them for him. They're trash." I throw them aside.

"I didn't wear them for him."

"Just like you didn't wear that ring for him. Don't move." I lift off of her, pressing my hand between her shoulder blades and smacking her backside again. She gasps and arches into the touch. "Did you let him do that to you? Did he figure out how much you like it?"

"Stop, Rick. Stop talking."

I push off the bed and unbutton my shirt just far enough to pull it over my head. She twists around to face me. I kick off my shoes and unbutton my pants. "Don't worry. I heard. You're on birth control." I finish undressing. By the time I'm done, she's naked and perfect, and pissed off, while my cock juts between us because I'm thick and hard and just as pissed off.

She's also sitting on the edge of the bed. "Are you serious right now, Rick? You left." She stands up.

I shackle her wrist and pull her to me. "I never gave a ring to another woman."

"Ten years."

"*Eight* fucking years."

"Does it matter? It was too long."

I catch her neck under her hair and drag her mouth to mine. "I know that. Do you not feel how much I know that? Do you know how many times I changed one decision because it meant life or death? Do you know why I did that? Because I needed one more chance with you."

"You took too long."

"Don't say that. Not if you mean it's too late. Tell me it's not too late."

CHAPTER TWENTY-ONE

Savage

I don't give her time to answer. I don't want the gutting reply to be delivered. "Don't answer," I say. "Because I know what you'll say now. I'm going to change your mind." I turn her, taking her down on the mattress, me leaning over her. "I'll pay for your anger in orgasms." I try to move away and she catches my neck.

"I don't want an orgasm—okay, that's not true—but that's not the point. I want you, Rick Savage. I've always wanted you. I *missed* you. I really did miss you." She says those words like they hurt. Because they do. She didn't want to miss me. She doesn't want to want me again. But it's something. I'll take anything I can get.

"I won't let you miss me again," I promise, fighting the demons in my head that scream: she'll wish you were gone again soon. She's not better without me, I remind myself. And I'm damn sure not better without her. "Of the many things I missed about you, baby," I say, "and there are so damn many things I missed about you, I missed you on my tongue."

"Rick," she breathes out. "Rick, I—"

"Don't talk. That's what you wanted, right?"

"I changed my mind."

"Later. *This* now." I kiss her jawline and then her neck, my breath warm on her skin as I whisper, "Candy on my tongue," repeating what I used to say to her, reminding her of all the things that make us, us. "I could lick you all night long." I fill my hands with her spectacular breasts, licking one of her puckered pink nipples. She gasps and arches into my hands. I have a moment when I think of that fucker Gabriel touching her like this and I want to punch something. Instead, I lick her nipple, suckle it deep and then I inch back upward to kiss her. "You're not marrying him."

"No. I'm not. But not because you're ordering me not marry him."

"Why?"

"Among other things, because I don't hate you."

"You don't hate me?" I repeat.

"That's all you get right now."

"All right. I'll take it. Say it again."

She lifts her head and kisses me and then says, "I don't hate you."

I kiss her, I kiss the hell out of her again, and I can feel a dark, raw need expanding inside me. A seed of something that I don't want to feel. That part of me that doesn't feel like I'm worthy of her. That part of me that knows my life is dangerous. That my life is not what she deserves. I don't want to feel those things. I don't want to go to that place now or ever again. She's not better off without me. She's not safer without me, a man who will kill for her, die for her.

Dragging my mouth from her mouth but not her perfect body, I start kissing a path downward. And she is perfect. She has always been my ideal woman, the one no one else lived up to. The one no one could ever make me forget. I kiss her belly and then drag her lower, to the edge of the mattress and I go down on one knee, spreading her legs wide. My lips return to her belly, my eyes meeting her eyes. She swallows hard and squeezes her eyes shut. I kiss my way downward, lower. Lower. My fingers slide between her legs, stroking the wet, slick heat there, my mouth lowering, tongue licking her clit. Her body jerks and arches upward. My hand slides under her backside and I squeeze at the same moment I suckle her deeply. I'm on a mission now, the taste of her, the soft, sexy sounds she's making, telling me where she needs me and I don't make her wait. Not this time. This time I want her to remember how good I can make her feel. She shatters on my tongue, the salty-sweet taste of her release on my lips, the shudders of her body beneath my hands. I bring her down, lick her until she's trying to sit up and then I'm up. I'm moving to the bed, taking her with me, rolling her to her side, to face me, settling my rock-hard cock between her thighs and tangling fingers in her hair, dragging her mouth to mine. Licking against her tongue before I murmur, "Taste yourself on my lips. That's where you belong."

I don't give her time to reply, closing my mouth over hers and cupping her as I stroke my cock along the seam of her sex, and press inside her. I groan with the feel of her around me, pressing deep, driving into her, and then settling in to stay right there. "It's been far too long since I was inside you, woman." My mouth closes over hers once more, and my hand catches her leg, angling her hips and thrusting.

She gasps but she's right there with me, arching into me, touching me. Trying to get closer and I want her closer. I cradle her against me, mold her breasts to my chest, her hips to my hips. Swaying until I roll her to her back and drive into her, catching her leg to my hip. I thrust again and again, but somehow when our mouths collide, we're on our sides, facing each other again, and the minute my hand covers her breast, she gasps into my mouth. She trembles in my arms, her sex spasming around me and I'm undone. I'm right there with her, shuddering with the intensity of my release.

When we finally still, I don't let her go. I hold onto her. I don't want to let her go. "Rick," she whispers.

I drag my hand through her hair and tilt her face to mine. "Yes, baby?"

"I—feel very confused right now."

"I don't. I'll help you find your way. There are so many things I need to say to you right now but," I stroke her lips, "you have to pee, don't you? You always have to pee after sex."

She rewards me with the laugh I'd hoped for, that soft musical laugh of hers, and runs her fingers over my goatee. God, I missed her doing that. "Yes," she concedes. "I do indeed need to pee. And *you* have to order pizza. You always have to eat after sex."

"Just like old times."

Pain slashes through her eyes. "I don't know if that's good or bad, Rick."

"It's good, baby. This, us. We're better than good. We're un-fucking-believable. Don't move. I'll grab you a towel."

"Okay."

Only I don't move. "You're not moving, Rick."

"No. No, I'm not, am I?"

She strokes my cheek. "I'm not going anywhere. It's my house."

Her house.

It was *our* fucking house.

"You're right. It's your house. I'll get the towel." I get up and grab my pants before I start walking toward the bathroom.

CHAPTER TWENTY-TWO

Candace

Rick walks in all of his buck-naked perfection toward the bathroom and disappears inside. I want to call him back. I want to lick him all over like he did me. I want to revel in all that muscle. I want to be back in the moment, back in his arms. Back in the middle of passion and escape, where tomorrow doesn't matter and neither does yesterday. I want my best friend back.

I roll and grab a box of tissues, clean up and sit there, staring at the door. Is he upset that I called this my house? I'm confused all over again, but hurt and anger stabs at me hard and fast. I grab his shirt because it's the first thing I can find, drag it around me, shove my arms in and roll the sleeves up. It smells all woodsy and wonderful like he does. I hug it around me, holding it close like I want to hold him. Like I want to hold onto the fantasy of all we once were and felt like again a few minutes ago. He's still not returned. Part of me wants him to want this to be his home. Part of me thinks he has a lot of arrogance to believe he can walk back in here and just expect that kind of welcome. I cling to anger because again, it's the safest emotion I have. It's like a shield. I need it to protect me from what's there brewing beneath my surface, ready to erupt.

I march to the bathroom and step inside the door to find him in his pants, leaning on the sink, chin to his chest, his powerful shoulders bunched up. Tattoos he didn't have before are etched down his arm and back. A skull in a Green Beret hat. I didn't even know he'd become a Green Beret. There's more, too, things I suspect represent parts of his life

I haven't known. He's different. He's not the man I knew. I know this, and yet I know him. "Are you really upset that I called this my house?"

He pushes off the counter and turns to face me, more ink down his chest that I hadn't noticed in the dark bedroom, his mouth on my body, and his body pressed to my body. A snake. A knife. "If I wasn't upset that you called it your house," he says, "then what would be the point of me being here right now?"

"You made it your house when you asked me for forever, Rick. You made it mine again when you said goodbye."

He steps toward me and I back away.

I point at him, a silent warning to stay where he's at in the action, warning bells and reality carving out a piece of me. "Why are you here?"

"For you," he says, his voice low and rough.

I shake my head, rejecting that idea. "There's more to it."

"Candace—"

It's not denial. I know him. Tattoos and years without me be damned, I do still know this man and I know what that means. "I'm right. You didn't come for me at all."

"I'm not leaving without you."

Words.

Words he feels he has to say, maybe he even wants to mean them, but he doesn't. I'm just a blast from the past that just happened to cross his path again. "Yes," I say. "Yes, you are leaving without me." I turn away from him, remarkably without tears. I've cried so many tears for this man. If I let myself cry for him again, I'll cry an ocean, and not one that turns to heat and passion. An ocean of pain and destruction. He's going to destroy me before this is over if I let him. Actually, I'm pretty sure I already have. I all but run out of the bedroom, toward the kitchen. I have to find my ring. And my phone. What if Gabriel called? What if he had someone check on me? What if he finds out about Rick? I've put my father at risk.

I cut down the hallway and into the kitchen where I scan the floor and go down on my knees to look under the cabinet. Rick is suddenly beside me, pulling me to my feet.

"Are you really looking for that damn ring? While wearing *my* damn shirt?"

"You wanted me to take it off."

"Only because I want you naked again."

"You're leaving. I'm here alone. I have to deal with things going on in my life right now. I have to deal with it now and in my way. And you have to leave."

He turns me and presses me against the island. "Because of him?"

"Because I am not a game for you to play when you happen to have a job that brings you here."

"That's not what this is." He presses his hands on the island on either side of me. "I came here because there's a situation I have to deal with, you're right about that, but I only came because you're here. Baby, I can't change the past. I know you think me leaving was selfish. What's selfish is me staying, but it happened. What I knew would happen if I saw you again. I can't walk away. I'm that selfish bastard that won't walk away again."

My chest tightens with emotion and I whisper, "How do I know that?"

"Because you know me. You know me like no one else has ever known me."

My hand goes to his arm, over his Green Beret tattoo. "I didn't even know you were a Green Beret."

"But you knew I was a killer?" he challenges. "I won't lie. I've done things I don't ever want you to know that I did, but I need you to know, I always thought they were for the right reasons."

"But they weren't?"

"No. No, they weren't. I'm not a gentle man. And yet, I'm yours. I will always be your man. Now you have to decide what to do with me." He cups my face and kisses me. "I have much to say to you and you to me, but—"

"But?"

"You have to pee. And I have to order pizza."

I laugh and I love that he makes me laugh. I love that this moment feels like *us*. "I—I really do." I give another choked laugh. "And pizza with you sounds really good."

"I need you to know that I will protect you. I need you to tell me what trouble you're in. And I know you are." He lifts me off the counter and kisses me. "I'll take care of it and you." He turns me to the doorway, and leans in to say, "For the record, I love the fuck out of you in my shirt." He smacks my backside and sets me in motion. I yelp and hurry forward, feeling more womanly than I have in a very long time, and while I could just leave on that high, I remember his father. I remember a man who never felt like he ever belonged, except with me, I thought. I stop at the doorway and decide right then that I love this man. Even if he hurts me again, I can't hurt him. I can't stand the idea of hurting him.

I turn to look at him. "It's always felt like our place." And remembering his hands on my backside earlier and his comment about what pleases me, I add, "And no one ever figured out what I like but you. *Just you*, Rick Savage." And with that, I leave the room.

CHAPTER TWENTY-THREE

Savage

I stare after Candace, a smile sliding onto my lips and then fading. Holy fuck, what am I doing? I'm every shade of wrong for her that exists. She should be running from me. I should be protecting her from a distance, then walking away again.

My cellphone rings in my pocket and I snake it out to find Adam's number on the caller ID. I punch the Answer button. "Talk to me."

"He's on the road, with his campaign manager cozying up to him in the backseat of the car. He's fucking her."

My eyes manage to shift to the floor and catch on the fucking engagement ring. I close the space between it and me, scooping it up. "Typical asshole. Buy her a big ring and he thinks he can stick it to another woman."

"We've documented his fun and games. Blake got pulled into a high-profile serial killer in New York City right now. He's pulled away from this. Asher is going to get cozy in his hotel, monitor Gabriel, and then start looking for links between Tag and Gabriel."

Blake's helping to catch a serial killer. If that doesn't drive home the fact that I'm working for the good guys, I don't know what does. But that doesn't make me one of them, I remind myself, which leads me to Adam's next question, "Any word from Tag?"

"Nada, but that doesn't surprise me. He's playing me, setting me up. He needs time to do that. I need us to figure out how before he shows his hand."

"Then you've decided you need us?"

"Yes, you sorry smart-ass motherfucker. I've decided I need you. Because of her."

He laughs. "Yeah well, everyone needs a sorry smart-ass motherfucker on their side. Anything you know that I need to know?"

"Not yet. More soon." I disconnect and stare at the ring, which is about three carats and ten grand. The one I got her was half a carat and fifteen hundred dollars. Thank fuck I have money now. I'll buy her a damn thirty thousand dollar ring. I take the one in my hand and toss it in the trashcan.

Candace's phone starts ringing in her purse. I don't even hesitate. She's in trouble. I need to know what the fuck is going on and I need to protect her. I grab it and glance at the caller ID that reads "Gabriel." I decline the call. He immediately sends a message: *Answer or I'll worry. You know I don't like to worry.*

I grimace and type: *You pea dick piece of shit.* My finger hovers over send but I'm reminded of the fear I've sensed in Candace. I need to know what's going on before I treat this dick like a dick. I grimace and delete the message before I type: *Throwing up. Millie is making me stay with her.* I hit send.

"Are you reading my messages?"

At Candace's voice, I look up to find her in the doorway and damn she's a sight for these deprived eyes. Her brown hair and green eyes coming together in a perfect pinup fantasy. One I've had a million times since foolishly leaving her behind. "Yes." I don't even consider lying. Lies are not what we need. Lies will destroy what's left of us. "Are you pissed?"

She crosses to stand in front of me, a sweet little sway to her hips, before she snatches her phone from my hands. "No. I suppose I should be, but I'm exhausted by anger right now." She glances at the message and then back at me. "I'm at my father's and throwing up."

"Brutally throwing up. It's disgusting. There's no possible way that bastard would want to stick his tongue down your throat. On the off chance he still tries, I volunteer to cut his tongue off."

SAVAGE HUNGER

She blinks up at me, the way she used to when I said over the top shit, and then also as she had in the past, she moves on. I love that shit. The way she acts like I said nothing outrageous. "I'll call Millie and make sure she backs me up."

"We need to talk about you and him."

"Did you order the pizza?"

"That's a change of topic I can't allow."

"Did you order the pizza?" she repeats.

"Not yet," I admit.

"Then we can't talk. I'm hungry. It needs to start working its way to us. And on that note, I'm calling Millie while turning on the fireplace. The house is cold." She walks toward the living room, those sweet hips swaying again. My cock standing up and paying her the attention she deserves.

I'm pussy whooped and I don't even give a fuck. I do as told. I dial the pizza place, and bingo, the number is still as good as my rock hard memory. Obviously, my cock is doing my thinking right now. Everything is rock hard. I'm so fucking rock hard.

I place the order, and with fucking on my mind, I walk into the living room, déjà vu slapping me hard in the face, a thousand memories crashing over me.

"Thanks, Millie," Candace says, settling onto the couch and grabbing a blanket. She always has a blanket on top of her that I have to fight to replace with me.

I sit down next to her, remembering our first night here, her naked and on that occasion, she was on top of me, while I was falling the fuck in love. "Same couch." I drag her legs over my lap. "It survived the years well."

"Better than me," she dares. "And you I'm not big on change."

"And yet you were wearing another man's ring."

"Really Rick? That's where you want to go? You left. You—"

"I know. Fuck. I'm sorry. That's wasn't fair."

"No. No, it wasn't fair."

"I threw the ring in the trash."

She gapes. "You did what? That's a ten-thousand-dollar ring."

127

"Fuck him and that ring. Why were you even wearing it?"

"Do you know how badly you deserve to hear: that's not your business?"

"I get it. I'm an asshole. I'm a prick. I'm a piece of shit. I'm the douche of douches. I also never even considered giving another woman a ring. Now, why were you even wearing his ring?"

"He asked."

"He asked?" I scowl in disbelief. "Are you fucking serious, woman? Is that your criteria because that isn't making me feel good about you saying you'd marry me."

"It's complicated."

I read between the lines and it's written in my regret and what she doesn't want to say to me. "You thought you loved him," I say flatly.

"No." She laughs bitterly. "No. You made sure that didn't happen." She shifts the topic back to me. "You really never—"

"Never. There's never been anyone for me but you."

"Yes, but—"

"No but. There's never been anyone but you. I won't tell you I didn't fuck my share of women. But that's all they were. That's all they were ever going to be." I lower my voice. "Candace, baby. I need you to talk to me about Gabriel. Why did you agree to marry him if you didn't love him?"

She seems to fret a moment and then she says. "It's easier to show you." She grabs her phone from where she's slipped it to the couch beside her and tabs to something she clearly plans to share. Just not yet. "I found a phone and didn't recognize it. I grabbed it and just started tabbing through it. I now believe it to be Gabriel's burner phone. The very fact that he needs a burner phone says a lot. This message was the message on it." She hands me her phone with a photo pulled up. I read the message:

The general has to go sooner rather than later, but after the wedding. I'm going to rush the proposal. That means you speed things up. He's becoming difficult. He needs to know that I can take everything from him, including her. If that doesn't work, we'll end him in a more final fashion.

128

Her father *was* Black Moon. He was the one who dictated the work to Tag for that project. It would be easy to assume that Gabriel has a link to that operation and wants anyone who knows about that link, dead. Maybe that's even why he sought out Candace. She completed his resume and controlled her father, or so he thought. No one controls her father. It would also, at this point, be easy to assume that's why Tag wanted me here. To kill Gabriel.

It would be a simple assumption, too simple.

There's something I'm missing.

CHAPTER TWENTY-FOUR

Savage

"He proposed three days after I found that message," Candace says, drawing me back to her and out of my own head. "I forced myself to say yes because I was afraid for my father. He's deployed. I couldn't contact him. I still can't. I'm afraid to even try. I have no idea who he can trust. I don't know who I can trust."

"Me," I say. "You can trust me."

"I do. I trust you. That's not what I meant, but no one else. He's powerful, Rick. His resources reach far and wide."

"As do mine, far more so than you realize right now." The doorbell rings and there is too much left to say, too much about the past that can't be said here and now, while our delivery waits. I'm not even sure it's territory you dive into while eating pizza. "Let's eat. Then we'll get into all of this. Are you okay with that?"

"I can't put him at risk."

"I'll protect your father. You have my word."

"Yes, but—"

I lean in and kiss her. "Right now, let's enjoy the first pizza we've shared in years together."

"Yes," she whispers and then with a firmer voice she adds, "Yes. Okay. I just—okay. I'd like that very much."

"I'll grab the pizza." I kiss her and shift her legs off my lap, standing up and walking to the door, zipping my pants as I go. I check the window and confirm there's no boogie man outside. Just a delivery kid in glasses with a nose ring. There's a story there. I just don't want to hear it. Regardless of the harmless kitten holding our pizzas, I still want my

131

damn guns and knives, which are in Candace's kitchen drawer where I put them when I arrived for good reason. I didn't want to freak her the fuck out. I open the door, grab our boxes, and send the kid on his way with a generous tip.

As much as I need to process what I now know, I don't linger by the door. I return to the living room. Candace is doing the same, returning from the kitchen with a couple of drinks in her hands. And damn, once again, all I can think is she's so fucking beautiful, her dark hair a mussed-up sexy mess that is all the sexier because I made it that way. We sit down on the sofa and I open the box, cheese bubbling around pepperoni. "I missed this place."

"I missed it with you," she says, sounding uncharacteristically shy.

Damn if I don't swell with emotions that I didn't even know I was capable of anymore. Over pizza. But it's pizza with her. It's memories with her. "I'm damn glad you did," I say, brushing fingers over her cheek, a moment between us that is all kinds of snap, crackle and pop. "If you keep looking at me like that I'm going to eat you instead."

Her cheeks heat and she grabs a slice of pizza. "Pizza first."

"You're barely convincing me," I warn her but I cave and grab a slice of pizza. I even change the subject from me between her legs, to her throughout the years. "Tell me about your job, baby. Have you built all you dreamed you would?"

"I still have a few things on the list. But I've made a real name for myself in military facilities."

"Tell me about it," I urge, and I want to hear. I want to know what I missed. I want to know what I should have been here to experience with her.

And she doesn't deny me my wish.

Her eyes light and she launches into a story about her first project and how it became career-making. Listening to her, I remember how her excitement about her career, and life in general, used to take me away from my troubles at home. How she made me want to wake up just to do this thing called life with her. "I'd like to see some of your work. All of your work. Which one is your favorite?"

"A building in New York City."

"Really? I live in New York. Which one?"

"The Penson Tower," she says, but her excitement is gone. Her expression tightens, right along with her voice. "You live in New York City?"

I've reminded her of the life I've lived without her, the one she thinks I chose over her. "Come there with me. Show me your building."

"I don't know." She looks down. "That feels impossible now."

I shut the pizza box we've all but emptied while talking. "It's not." I turn to face her, and catch her chin, angling her gaze to mine. "I will handle lying Gabe."

"It's not just about him. It's about us. You came home and it wasn't here."

"I was never home, until I came back to you."

"But you didn't."

"I had reasons. I needed to protect you. I didn't realize that I wasn't protecting you at all. So I say again: come to New York City with me. I'll take care of Gabriel."

"He's careful. He'll be hard to take down."

"Not careful enough," I assure her.

"You can't just kill him." She tries to get up and I catch her hand.

"Is that all you think I am? That' I'm a cold-blooded killer? Is that why you're not saying yes to coming to New York with me?"

"No. No, it's not."

I don't believe her. "The killer comment, Candace, it says otherwise."

"I didn't mean that. I just meant—he's high profile."

"If he wasn't, I could just kill him, right?"

"What are you doing, Rick?" she asks, her tone earnest. "What are you trying to prove right now? Because I don't deserve the way you're coming at me right now."

"You're right. You're right." I grab her hands and kiss them. "You're so fucking right. You don't deserve any of this." *Or me*, I think. That's been the problem all along.

"Don't do that. Don't start dividing us already. You're being defensive. You're creating a reaction in me that's not my own, deciding for me what my thoughts must be. You're making sure goodbye feels right again."

"No. I'm not. Or *fuck*. Maybe I am, but that's not what I want." I scrub a hand over my head and stand up, walking to the fireplace and pressing my hand on the wall. She has a right to know who she's in bed with. And she needs to know I can help beyond killing that sham Honest Gabe.

I turn to face her and she's sitting on the edge of the couch, her spine stiff, my shirt swallowing her. *My shirt.* I *want* her in my shirt, and the way that affects me, the way I feel right now when I'm with her, reminds me I am a man, not just a killer. "You deserve to know who and what I am."

"You want to scare me away," she accuses.

"I want you to know who I am."

"I know you became a mercenary, Rick. You know I know. I'm a general's daughter. I know what that means."

"You called me a killer," I remind her.

"I was hurt. I was angry. I didn't—"

"But I am. I *am* a killer. You weren't wrong, Candace. And your father told you for a reason. Because no father wants his daughter with the likes of me."

"He's protective," she murmurs softly. "He's supposed to be protective."

That confirmation that her father told her to stay away from me bites like a bitch. He pulled me into Tag's operation. He made me what I am right now. I could say that. I could make damn sure she knows the whole story but I do respect her father. I'll give him a chance to tell her first. And those facts do nothing to wash away the blood on my hands and that blood is a river. Fuck, it's an ocean.

I close the space between me and her, move the pizza box again and then sit on the table in front of Candace. She looks up at me with fucking love in her eyes. Love. Love that I don't deserve. Until that moment I'd thought to explain

134

myself to her. To tell her my story, but to what end? How the fuck do I justify cold-blooded murder?

I decide not to try. Her father doesn't want me in her life. Her father knows what he made me. I know, too. She's the only person in denial. Or maybe she's not. That "you can't just kill him" comment says otherwise.

"I'm a killer and you're too good for me," I say. "We're both living in a moment."

"Ah," she says, her voice cracking as she adds, "There it is. Faster than I expected. You're leaving."

"I'm not leaving. Not yet."

"Not yet?" she repeats. "Really, Rick? Not yet?" She shoots to her feet and I go with her. "Go now," she says, shoving on my chest. "I can deal with Gabriel on my own. I shouldn't have even told you."

I catch her arm and pull her to me. "That's not going to happen, because you see, baby, I was sent here to kill him. And I'm the only hope your father has of staying alive."

CHAPTER TWENTY-FIVE

Savage

Candace's stare burns into me, a hot flame scorching me with anger. "I knew you'd hurt me again. I just didn't know it would be this fast."

"I'm not hurting you, baby. I'm protecting you. From him and me."

"You're a dick."

"And a killer. You said so."

"That's not what I said."

"You said enough. There's a lot going on here you don't know about and too much that I don't know."

She shoves out of my arms. "I need you to leave."

"I'll sleep on the couch, but I'm not leaving."

"You can't just stay if I tell you that you can't stay."

"I am. I can. I will."

"Why? Obviously staying isn't your thing."

I all but flinch with that insult. "You are."

"Whatever, Rick. Am I in danger?"

"At this point, I don't believe you're in danger. No."

"But my father is?"

"I believe there's something your father knows that can hurt Gabriel. I believe he'd be willing to kill him to protect himself, yes."

"That's what I need to know. You don't have to stay. I'll do what you need me to do to protect my father."

"I'm staying. End of topic."

"Then I'm going to bed." She jerks at her arm and I let her go. "Without you," she adds.

"Smart decision," I say, and when she rushes out of the living room, she's leaves a trail of sweet smelling flowers that suffocate me in loss. Mine. I keep losing the one thing that matters to me. Her. She's what matters.

Fuck.

Fucking fuck. fucking *fuck*.

What did I just do?

What am I doing?

I walk into the kitchen, open the bar, and holy hell. She still has a bottle of whiskey that I bought. She never got rid of it. She let go. Not of me and not of the past. I want to roll around like a damn dog in the grass and revel in that realization, but I just made her hate me. Because I love her. Because she needs to hate me. I grab the bottle and open it, guzzling down a drink, letting it burn my throat. With the bottle still in hand, I walk to the drawer, pull out my gun and set it on the counter. Then I drink again before I remove my knives—three of them. Pretty and perfect, they can kill in three seconds flat. If well handled by a killing machine. That would be me. I know it. Candace knows it. Her damn father knows it. No reason to hide my weapons.

I set the bottle down and grab the counter. I told her I came here to kill Gabriel when I came here to kill Tag. I came here because he knows she matters to me, but I just made sure she doesn't. And I need to leave it at that. I have to leave it at that. I pull on my shoulder holster—fuck the shirt I'm not wearing—and once my gun is comfy at my side, I snap up the bottle again and walk back into the living room. I sit back down on the couch where Candace and I fucked the first time. Only it wasn't fucking. I made love to her. The only woman I've ever made love to in my entire blood-laced life.

I set down my gun and phone right in front of me on the table when my cell rings with Blake's name flashing on caller ID. I answer with, "I thought you were out catching serial killers or some shit like that?"

"I hope like fuck I am, but for now, I need to talk to you about Gabriel."

"I'm listening."

"Everything to do with your black ops project is completely un-hackable. There's not much I call impossible. This is."

"It went high up the government chain. You know I don't slaughter people for just anyone."

"Oh fuck. Are you drinking?"

"Fine whiskey, man."

"Well stop. Because this is the kind of top-secret shit that gets people killed, including your woman."

"I do my best fighting drunk and she's not my woman. She's just the woman I love."

"I won't touch that one with a ten-foot pole. Back to me. That seems a safer topic. Here's what I did. I managed to draw a time and communication line between Tag and his team and people in Gabriel's circle. Once Adam told me the general was a part of your operation, I included him. And fuck me, and all of us for that matter, considering how deep you are in this, there are links. Enough for me to believe this is all about that operation."

"Candace found a message on a burner phone," I say. "Once he marries her, he's going to deal with her father."

"Maybe he has a hit list that includes you."

"And Tag," I say. "No doubt that's why I'm here. To deal with him."

"Anything from Tag?"

"Nothing. I need to reach her father."

"I know. He's in a hot territory. I'm working on it. I'm working on ways to protect him. Don't kill Gabriel. That's not who you are with me."

"You sure about that?"

"I am. I think you need to get sure with me. He's corrupt. He's got people around him that are corrupt. Let's take him and them down. Protect the woman you love. I've got a serial killer to catch."

"If I were there, I'd kill him for you."

"In this case, I'd let you. Not Gabriel, Savage." He hangs up. I take another drink. My phone buzzes with a text from Asher. *I'm in place. And he's presently fucking his campaign manager.*

CHAPTER TWENTY-SIX

Candace

I wake alone in bed, with swollen eyes and the sound of rain pattering on the roof and splattering a song on my windows. Wonderful. It's raining. And rain reminds me of the night I met Rick. I loved rain from that moment forward, right up until the Dear Candace letter. Then it became pain. It made me think of Rick and all we had and lost. And it's pain now. He's here but he's not here for me. He was never here for me. He was here for Gabriel. *To kill* Gabriel. I sit up and grab my phone to read nine AM. There's no message from my doting fiancé—surprise, surprise, but there is one from Linda: *How are things?*

In other words, did I see Rick? Of course, I saw Rick. I not only saw him, I let him fuck me and break my heart again. I reply with: *Still mad at you. I'll think about calling you tomorrow.*

She replies with: *He's hotter than I remember.*

I reply with: *You are not getting me to talk about him.*

She replies with: *I'm coming over.*

I reply with: *Don't do that. I beg of you.*

Don't beg, Rick always says and yet he begged for trust. And then he turned on me. He's such an asshole. I throw away the blanket right as Linda replies with: *He's there, isn't he?*

I don't answer her. I stand up and stare at my body in Rick's shirt. Why did I leave it on? My gaze catches on his shoes and socks peeking from a spot at the end of the bed. He's somewhere in my house, that used to be *our* house, shoeless, sockless, and shirtless. Lord help me, this isn't getting any easier. I hurry into the bathroom, and with rough hands, slide out of his shirt, and climb in the shower. Forty-five minutes later, I've dried my hair, applied my make-up lightly, as I normally do, but with extra effort today to hide my puffy eyes. And my hair is no longer silk mahogany. It's a slightly frizzy brown. Apparently, my new "no frizz ever" product doesn't work. I look like crap. I look like the heartbroken ex who got played. Because I am and I did.

I dress in jeans that I pair with a pink fluffy sweater that I consider my comfort sweater for no reason other than it just is. It's also not sexy at all. It's big. It shows nothing. It most assuredly does not say: I slept in your shirt last night and want to have sex with you again despite knowing you're an asshole. It says: not feeling it. Which is good. Because I *do not* want to have sex with Rick Savage *ever again*. And not because he's a killer. Because he really is an asshole. Who is also really good with his mouth. A memory of him between my legs has me groaning. Oh good Lord. I'm a fool over this man.

Shoving away that self-destructive thought, I focus on protecting my father. I don't know what Rick is going to do besides kill Gabriel, which should freak me out, but I seem to be numb. All of this feels impossible, like a bad dream, but I can't live in that space or this bedroom. I have to go out there and face Rick Savage, and the challenges before me. But I also need to count on me and my plan. I need that ring to be back on my hand. I need to stay my path with Gabriel until I can talk to my father.

I hurry through the bedroom, exiting while steeling myself for a half-naked hot man I'll be forced to encounter, my heart thundering in my chest. Once I reach the kitchen, it's empty and a peek in the living room says it is as well. I stand there listening, with no sound but the ticking of the clock on the wall. He's not here. He left. Hugging myself, I fold forward with the blow of this realization. He's gone. I should be happy. A killer that used me and hurt me is gone. But I don't know if I'll ever see him again and that is almost unfathomable. I let the brutal stab of pain become anger and set myself in motion. I need to dig that ring out of the trash. I need to start thinking about what comes next.

I hurry into the kitchen to find a pot of fresh coffee. What a jerk. He had coffee before he left. Of course. Why wouldn't he? He had me, too, spread wide and moaning. Why not my coffee? I open the trashcan to find the bag missing. Oh my God. *Oh my God*, no. I rush to the garage door and yank it open, to still at the sight of a black Porsche sitting in my garage. A very expensive black Porsche at that.

"I made a lot of money killing people."

At Rick's voice, I turn to find him standing a few steps from me. I whirl on him and yank the door shut behind me. And I don't know how he did it, but the big brute of a man is in black jeans, a black T-shirt, and boots. And that scar on his face screams of a life and secrets I don't know and will never know. It taunts me the way he's taunting me right now, and I'm officially at my limit, a limit that's been building for weeks with the men in my life. I lose it. I make some animalistic sound that I don't even recognize as my own and launch myself at him.

He catches me before I do any damage and then next thing I know I'm pressed against the wall, his big body caging mine.

"What are you doing, woman?" he demands.

"I'm tired of being played with. I can't take it. First Gabriel. Now you. I can't take it. Are you going to kill me, too? Is that what this is?"

He blanches. "You think I'd kill you?"

"Isn't that what you want me to think? You're a killer. You made a lot of money killing people. What do you want from me, Rick?"

Suddenly his hand is under my hair, cupping my neck and he's dragging my mouth to his. "What I can't have. What I've always wanted. *You*." His mouth closes down on mine, his tongue pressing long and deep, drugging me, demanding my response.

I fight to resist. I do, but the taste of him—coffee with some kind of sweet creamer mixed with man—and the woodsy scent of his cologne, undoes me. I moan and sink into the kiss, angry with myself for my weakness. Angry at him for bringing it out in me. But anger doesn't stop the pain or the absolute hunger for Rick Savage. I will always love him as much as I hate him. The hate is what reminds me of how mean he was last night. About how easily he left me alone in that bed. He hadn't slept with me in all those years and he chose the couch over me. I shove against him.

"Stop," I gasp. "Stop now." I shove on his chest. "Is this what you want? To hurt me? To confuse me? To punish me?"

"I'm trying to protect you."

"If this is you protecting me, then you might as well be killing me slowly and painfully. You're the killer who loved me and left me. I guess I should count my blessings. I'm not dead yet."

"You know I wouldn't hurt you. I'd kill for you, woman."

"Die for me, but carve my heart out of my chest? Those things don't compute. Last night hurt me. The Dear Candace letter hurt me. You excel at hurting me."

The doorbell rings and his jaw clenches. "That will be my men. They're here to help us—"

"There is no us, Savage. That's what you wanted. Just tell me what you need from me because we both know that's why you're here. You don't just want to kill Gabriel. You want me to help you."

CHAPTER TWENTY-SEVEN

Candace

Torment slides across Rick's face, but after last night, I'm done trying to save him. The doorbell rings again and I push on his chest. "Just get this over with and tell me what you need from me."

"Hating me is the safest thing you can do," he says, and with that, he steps away from me and walks toward the front of the house.

I suck in a breath with the confirmation that he might be here now, but not for long. He's done with me. He's been done with me and this is the reality check I need. I need to be done with him as well. Determined to move to that place, I calmly walk to the coffee pot, fill a cup and add Splenda and creamer. Voices sound in the living room and I move in this direction.

I turn and lean on the counter as Adam enters the kitchen with another tall, brown-haired man by his side. Both men have on jeans and T-shirts. "Morning, Candace," Adam greets.

"Morning," the other man says, offering me a two-finger wave. "Name's Smith."

"Morning, and I'd say nice to meet you, but I don't know if it is. However, you're both welcome to coffee if you like." Rick walks into the room, his eyes intense as they meet mine, and I add, "Savage made the coffee so I don't promise it won't kill you."

Adam whistles. "Savage, not Rick, and an assassin joke. Ouch. I guess I know how things are going between you two."

"There are three kinds of creamers in the fridge," I say, ignoring his remark, and when they both move in my direction, I add, "Mugs are above the pot." I head for the exit and the living room, which forces me to walk right by Rick. He catches my arm, heat radiating up and across my chest, damn him.

"Candy—"

"Candace," I correct, meeting his stare, letting him know that I might be puffy-eyed today, but I'm fighting for me and my father today, not him. "Always Candace to you. And this kitchen is too small for all of us." I pull my arm from his grip. "I'll be in the living room when you're ready to tell me what you want from me." I hurry forward, somehow both relieved and destroyed, when he lets me go.

Me and my mug walk to the living room, where I find several soft leather briefcases on the coffee table. I walk past them and to the window, where I pull back the curtain and watch the rain fall steadily to the ground. Perpetual rain. The way Texas relieves the heat, but considering the simmering heat in my belly and the burn of my lips, there is apparently no relieving the heat Rick Savage stirs in me. Not even his promise to leave again.

"Good coffee," Adam says from behind me.

I turn to find him alone, and settling on the big chair I love beside the couch. The one I've fucked Rick in a hundred times. I wonder if he'd still sit there if he knew that? I think I need new furniture. If I live through this, I'll go shopping. "What do you need from me?"

"Trust," Adam says. "We're going to help you."

"Amen to that," Smith says, joining us. "That bastard can't be president." He sits down on the couch. "We aren't letting that happen."

"So, kill him and stop him?" I ask. "Is that the plan?"

"Kill him?" Adam laughs. "That's not what we do at Walker Security. Unless they shoot first. Then we shoot last."

I blink, thinking of several Walker Security signs at airports and military facilities. "I know that name. You do military contracts? And airports, too, right?"

"Our toes tap the water of many oceans," Smith says.

Adam gives him an incredulous look. "Our toes tap the water of many oceans? What the fuck?" He looks at me. "He sounds like Savage and all of his stupid sayings. Did you drug the coffee?"

"Ask Savage. He made it, remember?" And he's right. Rick says funny, nonsensical things that I love. Or used to love. "Where is he?"

"He's out back on the patio watching it rain with excessive interest," Adam replies. "He seemed to need to cool off. You both did." He motions to the chair on the other side of the table. "Can I talk you into sitting down and talking to me?"

I think I like Adam. Maybe. We'll see. I close the space between us and sit down, sipping my coffee, and to my horror, my hand trembles. Smith sets his mug down. "Relax. We're friends. I don't know what is up with Savage and what he told you, but I should kick his ass right now based on your nerves."

"Savage and I are complicated."

"To say the least," Adam agrees. "So let's focus on the simple stuff. Let us start by telling you about us. As you know I'm an ex-SEAL. Team Six. So is Asher, who isn't here now, because he's in Austin, monitoring Gabriel."

"He is?" I ask, surprised. "You have someone monitoring Gabriel?"

"He is," Adam confirms. "And we do."

"I'm an ex-Ranger," Smith replies, "though my background is a bit more complex than that or I wouldn't be with Walker. No one at Walker is just a soldier. We're ex-CIA, FBI, you name it. We're packed with alphabets and diverse skills."

"CIA?" I ask. "Like Gabriel?"

"Yes," Adam confirms. "Unfortunately, a few of our top ex-CIA operatives are in Europe on assignment, but we've got one of our newer men, en route now. New to us, but a seasoned pro. His name is Aaron. We feel like we need someone like him here helping us and you. We're the good guys. I'm proud of the men I work with and the jobs I do for Walker."

"I'm very confused right now. Why are you involved?"

"Because Savage is involved."

"And that happened how?"

"That's between you and Savage," Adam replies.

"Of course it is," I say.

"There's a lot going on here that Savage really needs to explain but here's what is cut and dry: we're here to protect you. We're here to protect your father. Those things are absolute. I'm sure Savage told you we have a man trying to get eyes on your father, to confirm his safety and offer him protection."

"No. No, he didn't tell me. All he told me was that he was here to kill Gabriel."

"That is not why he's here," Smith says. "That asshole." He eyes Adam. "What the fuck is he doing?"

Adam sets his mug down and leans forward, elbows on his knees. "He's let you believe he's nothing but a killer, hasn't he?"

"He seems to want me to believe that, yes."

"Let's talk about how I met him. I was in Saudi Arabia under fire."

"Stop talking, Adam."

At Rick's voice, my gaze lifts to find him standing in front of the table, between me and Adam, facing Smith. And he looks like he's about to blow, his eyes sharp, his jaw set hard, his fingers curled into his palms at his sides.

"I'm not going to stop fucking talking, Savage," Adam says, standing up, tall and broad, his actions daring Rick to come at him. "I know you think you're protecting her by making her think you're a killer."

"I *am* a killer. Nothing you're about to tell her changes that." He looks at me. "Nothing he tells you changes that."

"You had reasons for everything you did," Adam argues.

"You have no idea what you're talking about, asshole," Rick snaps. "You need to shut the fuck up."

"You think she's better off scared and hurt by the man she loves? She's captive to Gabriel, who's powerful, with CIA

SAVAGE HUNGER

operatives as skilled as you and me at his beck and call.
Think about it, Savage. You didn't even tell her you were
trying to protect her father."

"She was asleep." He doesn't look at me.

"She looks wide awake to me," Adam snaps back. "I'm
telling her. If you want to fight me first, so be it. But bloody
and bruised, I'm still telling her."

I shoot to my feet. "If he doesn't want me to know, Adam,
don't tell me. He wants to be a monster. He'd obviously
rather you be my hero. Anyone but him. He's made that
clear. And I don't need a hero. I need a problem I can help
solve."

CHAPTER TWENTY-EIGHT

Candace

Rick doesn't look at me. He glares at Adam and then turns away, walking to the fireplace and giving us his back. Defeated, I sink into the chair again. Adam sits back down, too, and looks at me. "Back to Saudi," he says, clearly listening to neither me nor Rick. He's going to tell this story. And I don't stop him. I don't understand what happened between Rick and I in the past or in the past few hours. I need to understand. "A portion of Walker's operation is high-risk missions," he continues. "A majority of us take them when we're new to Walker and while we're single for one reason: we get massive paydays. I took a job to save a princess from a bastard who had her and another woman captive. The contractor had paid us *and* the operation Savage worked for to do the same job. I'm telling you this because I was competing for Savage's payday."

Savage curses under his breath. "This means nothing," he says, turning around, his hands settling on his hips. "I was just staying alive."

Adam ignores him. "I took a life-threatening bullet. Savage operated on me while firing on the enemy. He saved my fucking life and saved the woman. He took me home to New York, met my boss, and we recruited him away from the bastard he was working for. That was the closest to dead I've ever been." He points at Savage. "That bastard there saved me. He's a hell of a surgeon and warrior. And he's my fucking friend."

Rick runs his hand over his head and eyes the ceiling with such intensity it seems like he's studying a hole that isn't there. Meanwhile, I still feel like shit. If Rick's a good, honorable man, why push me away for reasons aside from just not wanting me or us?

"Are you here to kill Gabriel, Savage?" I can't call him Rick. We're clearly beyond that. I'm like everyone else now. And everyone else calls him Savage.

His hands go back to his hips. "I didn't lie to you. I came for you."

I stand up and face him. "You *didn't* come for me. Why are you here?"

"Tell her," Adam orders. Rick doesn't speak and Adam adds, "He not lying. He came for you." He eyes Rick. "I know this is the part you don't want to tell her, but you have to tell her. *Tell her.*"

My heart starts to race. "Tell me what?"

Rick grimaces. Adam grimaces. "I'll tell her," Adam says. "He was a Beret and not just any Beret."

"That has nothing to do with why I'm here," Rick snaps.

"It has everything to do with why you came. She needs the history. And holy hell man. Stop playing the martyr. That's not you. You own who you are. You tell the world to fuck off all the damn time. Why can't you tell her who you are? She needs to know. She needs to trust you. She deserves that comfort right now. Even Asher hated you until he knew your story."

"Asher and I are more complicated than that and you know it."

"Because he thought he knew who, and what, you were," Adam snaps before fixing me in a stare. "They pulled him into a special unit, finished his surgical training and then took all of that skill and did a shitty thing. They made him an assassin for a black ops operation."

I glance at Rick. "That's how it happened?"

His jaw clenches. "Yes."

I want to ask when he decided to send me that letter but I settle on, "Then how did you end up a mercenary?"

"New president," he says, surprising me by actually answering. "The program funding was officially killed. Unofficially, it continued."

Adam jumps in again. "Someone he respected and trusted asked him to join the mercenary operation to keep it going the right way."

My eyes go wide and shoot to Rick. "Did you? Did it?"

"I didn't have any control," Rick says. "After enough kills, I drank my way through the rest of those years."

"Which is how we ended up here," Smith says. "Or that's what I hear."

My brow furrows. "I don't understand. What does that mean?"

Rick scowls in Smith's direction and then looks at me. "I put you at risk."

"I don't understand. How?"

"Vodka was my friend when I was working for Tag. He's the head of Dark Zone, the mercenary operation. I said some things."

"He talked about loving you and losing you," Adam supplies. "He's good at that. He drinks vodka. He talks about you. The next morning, he doesn't remember anything but you. You don't talk about what you love to a man like Tag. Savage gave Tag his weakness, which is you."

My gaze shoots to Rick. "Is that true?"

"It's true," he confirms. "I fucked up."

He fucked up, but he loves me. He's always loved me. I'm ridiculously relieved by this considering where we were last night and where we seem to be headed.

"Tag came to see me in New York," Rick explains. "He told me I owed him a favor. He's right. I do. In mercenary language, that's nothing you ignore. It's a blood oath. You pay up or you, and those you love, get hunted."

Understanding hits me. "You came for me, to keep me from being hunted."

"Yes. One more kill and I'm free of him. He told me I'd enjoy this one, too, but didn't give me the name. And then he told me to come here and wait for details. I knew the location wasn't a coincidence."

Smith interjects there. "We have reason to believe that Gabriel was a part of the black ops operation Rick was working for. And while he was CIA despite many of those operations being conducted on US soil."

"And it's illegal for the CIA to operate on US soil," I say. "Maybe my father found out what he did. Maybe Gabriel sees him as a threat to his presidency." I look at Rick. "You know, too. What if Gabriel hired Tag? What if they want you to kill Gabriel before he kills you?"

"Tag might well want me dead," Rick says, "but Gabriel didn't hire Tag. He might have tried but Tag isn't that stupid. Tag was a key player in that black ops program. He'd have dirt on Gabriel like no one else would. If Gabriel wants anyone gone, it's Tag. And Tag won't sit back and wait for an attack. He goes for the throat. That's his way. He kills you. Before you kill him. And so, he sent me."

"To kill Gabriel," I say. "It makes sense. Maybe he plans to use me as leverage. You kill Gabriel and I survive. Someone else does it and I don't?"

"We don't know that," Smith interjects. "Tag hasn't given him his orders. Everything is an assumption."

I blanch. "He hasn't given you the target?"

"He hasn't," Rick confirms. "But it's Gabriel. I'd bet my right arm on it."

I frown. "I feel like I'm missing something." I try to put it all together. "If Gabriel doesn't know you, why pursue me? It can't be a coincidence that he chose me, when I was engaged to you in the past. And I can't believe he chose me to control my father. My father would have warned me away from him."

Rick's lips thin. "The way he warned you about me?"

"He obviously didn't know your story, Rick. And he must not have known Gabriel's until I was already involved with him."

"Right," Rick says, motioning to the table. "Let's dig in and find the dirt on Gabriel to put him in jail." He walks to the table, grabs one of the briefcases and moves to a chair by the fireplace. He doesn't look at me.

There's something I still don't know. Something Rick still doesn't want to tell me. Something that not even Adam dares to push him to reveal.

CHAPTER TWENTY-NINE

Savage

I sit in that chair and will myself to stay in it.

Let's dig in and find the dirt on Gabriel to put him in jail.

Who the fuck even said that? Am I a boy scout now? No. I'm not. Nor have I ever been a fucking boy scout. I don't want to dig in and put Gabriel in jail. I want to dig his grave and shove him inside. And her father damn sure knows who and what I am. He created me.

He obviously didn't know my story, my ass. Holy fuck, I've tried to spare Candace her father's involvement in all of this, but right then, I wanted to tell Candace *he* created me. He molded me. He made me. But telling her that right now, while pissed off, would be like jamming a square into a circular hole. I'd make it fit but it would be painful as fuck.

Thus the boy scout shit that spewed from my mouth.

"So that's the plan?" Candace challenges. "Put him in jail?"

I glance over at her, my defenses prickling like Spidey senses. "Would you rather me kill him?"

"I don't think you can do that," she says primly.

I arch a brow. "And why is that?"

"You're acting like such an ass," she says, "that I'm going to kill you before you get the chance."

Adam and Smith laugh and just that easily, she's smashed my anger. God, I love this woman and as much as I'm pissed at Adam for telling my story for me, he was right. With all she's got going on, with all she has to fear, she needed to hear it. That's in the air right fucking now. "Is that right?" I challenge.

"Oh, it's so right," she assures me. "Stop acting like a little bitch." And then she snubs me with a look at Adam. "What can I do to help?"

"Just to be clear," I say, "she's the only one who gets away with that. And that's because she smells pretty. You two bastards might act pretty, but you don't smell pretty."

Adam leans toward her with a conspiratorial reply. "Don't kill him yet. We need him to make contact with Tag. In the meantime, you can look through the documents we pulled from Gabriel's hard drive."

"Oh," she says. "You pulled documents from his drive? You're very resourceful."

"You have no idea just how resourceful," Adam assures her.

"That's comforting," she says. "Because Gabriel was so high up the CIA ladder that his resources run deep. Especially overseas, where my father is now."

"We're there," I quickly assure her and when she looks at me, I add, "We'll get to him. We'll protect him, but based on that text you copied and showed me, he's safe for now. Gabriel wants you locked in before he goes after your father."

She nods. "I should call and check on him. I need to make him feel like I'm still all in."

My jaw clenches and the rejection is on my tongue when Smith jumps in with, "She's right. I'm reading through data on this guy. He's a bastard."

I cut my stare and grind my teeth so damn hard that my jaw locks up.

Candace angles in my direction. "It's to protect my father, Rick," she says. "And you. We don't know that he's not coming for you."

But we do because her father was the man giving us orders. If the CIA was involved, it was with him, not me. "He thinks you're sick. Shouldn't he be checking on you?"

"His affection for me, or lack thereof, is not in question," she says. "I just want to buy us time to do whatever we can do to protect my father."

My lips thin. "Text," I say. "You're on edge. He's going to know. He'll read it in your voice."

"He doesn't read anything from me," she says. "But I'll text." She grabs her phone, types the message, and then waits. Her phone buzzes back with a message and she reads it out loud: *In meetings. I'll try to call you in a few hours.*

Her eyes meet mine, and there's uncertainty and confusion in her stare. She doesn't understand why I'm so damn possessive and yet I shoved her away last night. Or why Adam had to tell her my history. I think of her words "you can't just kill him" again and cut my stare. That's who she believed I was before Adam told her otherwise. That's who her father told her I was. Fuck, that's who I told her *I* was. Why am I pissed that she believed me?

A few minutes later, we all have MacBooks in front of us reviewing copies of the same documents. In the hours that follow, I stick to my chair, keep to myself, but I can feel her sneaking looks at me, willing me to close the space between us, but I don't. If I go to her, I'm going to kiss the hell out of her, and she's going to end up naked, and on my tongue, again. And that won't happen without some potential shouting on her behalf that I probably, most likely, almost certainly, deserve.

CHAPTER THIRTY

Savage

Hours tick by filled with research and at some point, Adam pulls out a collage of photos that Blake sent him. Candace manages to identify a man we all feel might connect the dots we need connected. I weed through document after document with not much success. "I should search my father's home office," Candace offers. "Maybe there's something there that tells us what he knows about Gabriel."

"I did," I say. "Last night while you were sleeping."

She blanches and turns to me. "Did you find anything?"

"Nothing that helps," I say tightly.

"Maybe I'll see something you didn't."

She's right. She might. But that brings us back to her father's involvement.

The doorbell rings with a pizza order Adam insisted on half an hour ago . "I'll grab it," she says, standing up, allowing me a save that won't last.

Smith pushes to his feet. "I'll help."

The two of them leave and Adam and I are alone. "Better she finds out from you than Gabriel."

"You mean, better I tell her before it explodes from your Texas-sized mouth."

"You'll thank me for what I did later," he assures me. "I know you think you're protecting her by pushing her away, but you're a Walker now."

"Says the man that's here because Tag pulled me into this shit."

"Her father drug you into this shit and we're going to end it. We'll get you your freedom."

159

My enemies run deep, in a way his boy scout ass can't understand.

Smith and Candace return with a stack of pizzas. "We'll set them all out in the kitchen," Candace says and when she walks by, I have this caveman urge to chase her, throw her over my shoulder, and take her to the bedroom. When we're naked, all the rest of this shit burns away while we burn alive.

Adam's cell buzzes with a text and he glances at it and then me. "Aaron's flying in tonight. He says he has information we need that's better shared in person. And to watch our backs."

"I don't trust the CIA."

"He's not CIA. He's Walker."

"Once a CIA asshole, always a CIA asshole."

"Once a mercenary, always a mercenary?" he challenges.

"Exactly."

"We need him," he says, ignoring my reply. "And the CIA burned him, which is why he ended up with us. He knows how to rip through their secret chains of command."

"Gabriel was top-level CIA," I say. "They say it comes from above and flows down. That's Aaron's resume." I stand up. "Pizza calls." I walk toward the kitchen.

"Tell her," he calls out.

I lift a hand and enter the kitchen to find Smith and Candace laughing while eating pizza.

Thunder rumbles above and Candace jolts, her eyes rocketing to mine. "I guess I'm more uneasy than I realized."

"A little rain never hurt anyone," I say, my eyes meeting hers, the memory of the night we met in my mind, and the rain that gave me an excuse to scoop her up and put her in my truck. "I love a good rainstorm."

"I used to," she says softly.

I arch a brow. "Not anymore, though?"

"Not for a long time."

Adam squeezes past me, breaking the moment, with a forceful, "Bring on the pizza."

Everyone digs in then, loading up plates before we all end up at the kitchen table. I don't even hesitate to claim a spot next to Candace. I want to be near her. Hell, I want to be with her, so fucking badly, it hurts. Smith is the one who gets everyone talking. "Remember that time Adam disguised himself as an old pizza delivery man?"

"You did what?" Candace asks.

"He's a master of disguise," I say. "A beanstalk that can become a molehill. He's a freak, I tell you."

"That's what she said," Adam jokes, wiggling his eyebrows.

Smith groans at the bad joke and Candace delivers unto us, a perfectly sweet, girly laugh.

"An absolute freak show," I amend, taking a bite of pizza.

"He was all hunched over and still taller than everyone else," Smith laughs. "But that wrinkly face he wore? Fuck, man. That looked real. And the clown. The clown was freaky."

"Why were you a clown?" Candace asks.

"Because the guy I was hunting was afraid of clowns."

Candace laughs and God, I love her laugh. If I could bottle it, I'd drink it, snort it, lick it—no, I'd rather lick her. My mind goes to me between her legs last night and I stand up. "I need another slice."

"I need to make some calls," Adam says, while Smith, quiet mofo that he is, just gets up and says nothing.

"Just put your plates in one of the boxes," Candace says. "The trash bag is missing, thanks to Rick."

Adam and Smith get lost and then it's just me and her. I open the pizza box and we both reach for the last piece of pepperoni. "Mine," she teases as we both hang onto it.

"You know I've killed men for less," I say before I can stop myself.

The air is instantly charged and she lets go of the pizza, but her hand settles on my arm. "You're going to have to let go of the pizza to kiss me, you know that, right?"

I let it go and my hands come down on her arms, a million reasons to walk away from her in my mind and I want to reject them all. She smells good. She tastes good. She makes me feel good as fuck. "Candace—"

"I don't care about you being a mercenary. That's where life took you. And now it brought you back here."

Where life took me. Here it is. My moment has arrived. This is where I should tell her how it took me there. This is where I should explain how deep the connection between me and her father truly runs. "I need air," I say, setting her away from me and walking toward the patio door. I make it all the way there and stop. I'm shutting her out because I don't want to hurt her. I've spent eight years shutting her out and it didn't get me what I wanted which is her.

I glance over my shoulder to find her standing with her back to me. "Candy," I say softly.

She whirls around to face me, pain in the depths of those green eyes. "Yes?"

"Come with me." I exit the house and leave her to make the decision to follow.

CHAPTER THIRTY-ONE

Savage

I step onto the enclosed porch that I built years ago and press my hands to the railing, watching the rain drizzle onto the lawn, memories pounding at me. We'd been so damn in love and her father had been everything to me that mine had not been, a man I respected. A man I wanted to impress and make proud.

"Rick."

I turn toward Candace's voice, and the minute I see her standing there in that big pink fluffy sweater, I'm hot and hard, and in love in a way I wouldn't have believed possible if I hadn't met her all those years ago. I don't hesitate. I close the space between us, pull her to me, and fold her close. My hand goes to the back of her head, her back to the post behind us and my mouth to her mouth. I kiss her. I kiss her like I'm dying and she's the only life that exists. I kiss her and kiss her some more, and when finally I come up for air, the rain pounds down behind us, falling hard and fast, thunder rolling above.

"I'm going to protect you," I vow. "No matter what I am, who I am now, I will protect you."

Her eyes sharpen on my face. "You blame yourself. You think I'm going to blame you for putting my father at risk. You didn't cause this. You didn't make Gabriel do bad things."

My spine goes stiff and I release her, stepping away, pressing my hands back to the railing, battling between protecting her from her father's involvement and the necessity for her to know all in order to protect herself. In that moment, I do a silent "thank fuck" for Adam running his mouth. Because if I was a monster of her father's creation, her father is a monster, too. I can't do that to her. I can't make us that while she's engaged to that bastard.

"I should just go inside," she says, and I turn and catch her to me again, turning her back to that banister and setting my hands on her shoulders.

"Adam didn't tell you everything," I say.

"Are you going to tell me?"

"Unfortunately, yes."

"Whatever it is—"

"We need to talk about the man who pulled me into the black ops program. The man who convinced me to join the mercenary operation."

"You respected him."

"Very much and I wanted to protect him, I still do. For you, Candace."

Her brow furrows. "I don't understand."

"It was your father."

"What? *My father*?"

"Yes, baby. He gave the orders. I don't know how Gabriel fits into that, but I know he does. We've found enough for me to believe he wants those who could hurt him, Tag and your father, gone."

"My father turned you into an assassin."

"Your father saw something in me and exploited it. He didn't make me an assassin. I made me an assassin."

"How did he see an assassin in a surgeon?"

I release her and press my hands to the railing on either side of her. "A man who knows how to save a life knows how to take one." I push back intending to give her space to breathe, but she grabs my arm.

"Rick—"

I don't want to know what she's going to say. I catch the back of her head and kiss her, a deep stroke of the tongue that leaves no room for words. That's when the doorbell rings. Her hands go to my chest, urgency in her face, in her words. "What if Gabriel knows I'm not at my father's? What if Gabriel sent someone to check on me?"

My hands come down on my arms. "Relax, baby. We're watching him and you here. Maybe it's Linda."

"Yes. She texted me."

The patio door opens and Smith pokes his head out. "It's a sixty-something man in uniform."

"I don't know who that could be," she says, and then she pales, all the blood running from her face. "Oh God. *Oh God.* What if my father is dead? Are they informing me that my father is dead?"

"Candace, baby. No. They come in pairs. And it's usually young soldiers given that duty."

"Not always. Not always. That's not true." She twists away from me and charges at Smith, who moves out of the way.

She runs forward, and I quickly pursue. Her father isn't dead. That's not what this is. I'm sure of it for many reasons, including that text she found on Gabriel's burner phone. I catch up with her at the door, and she's facing me and leaning against it, looking pale. "It's not about my father, Rick."

I step in front of her. "Who is it?"

"Your father."

CHAPTER THIRTY-TWO

Savage

I lean forward, hands on the door on either side of her, my chin to my chest with the impact, the absolute fucking punch that is my father's visit. "What the fuck is he doing here?"

Candace's hands go to my face and she leans in close, her lips at my ear. "I can get rid of him."

Her reaction tells of how rich and deep our history runs. It's why she warned me about him at the event. She knows how I feel about him and she knows why.

"No," I say, lifting my gaze to hers and catching her hands between us. "He's a problem that gets in the way, our way. He needs to go away and stay away. I'm the one that makes that happen." I kiss her hands, a silent thank you in the action. "I got this."

"I don't want you to have to talk to him. I know what he does to you. We both know that he played as much of a role in why you left as anyone."

My hands come down on her shoulders. "I'm not the man I was then. No one controls what I do, especially that bastard. Go help Adam and Smith." I kiss her and set her away from me.

"Rick," she pleads, but I don't turn back. I open the door and step out onto the porch, pulling the door shut behind me.

My father straightens to damn near attention. "Son. I knew you'd be with her. I saw you with her last night. That politician she's engaged to has nothing on you."

That's a dig. He's rubbing in what I loved and lost. If I expected to feel something other than hate for the man, he's made sure I don't. I still hate him. "What do you want?"

"To see my son. You look good." His gaze slides to my cheek. "Except your face. I hope you hurt the man who did that to you."

"I killed him. What else?"

"Seriously? You haven't seen me in eight years and that's all you have to say?'

"We said all we had to say the night mom died."

"You haven't changed, I see. An arrogant, treacherous bastard." He laughs. "Chip off the old block."

"I am nothing like you."

"You're right. You're at the house of the future first lady, fucking her because you think you have the right. Not even I have balls that big."

He's baiting me. I'm not playing that game. I give him a smirk in return. That's all. I smirk and say nothing.

He laughs. "Ah, son. You are something else. Why don't you come out to Fort Sam and show me how you handle a scalpel these days?"

I close the space between me and him. "I'm not going anywhere with you, but let me be clear: if you speak one word about me being here—"

"You'll kill me?" he challenges. "Yes, I heard you became a killer."

He's the fucking killer, and there's a part of me that wants to ram him against the banister and punch him. But we've been there. I let him get to me and I went there. I'm not giving him that control again. "Glad we're clear then," I say, and I turn for the door.

My hand is on the handle when he says, "No threats. No harsh words."

I rotate and glance at him. "There's a difference between you, a surgeon, and me, an assassin. Your patients live to sing your praises. Mine do not." I open the door and enter the house, shutting the door behind me.

Candace is waiting, stepping in front of me, her hands on my hips. "What happened?"

"He's gone."

"I know that, but—"

"He's gone. Leave it at that."

She swallows hard. "Right. Shut up and let you deal with it your way. Which is always leaving." She tries to turn away and I catch her arm and turn her to me. "Don't do that. I just need to process."

"And I need to figure out what my father knows about Gabriel. Let go."

"Candace—"

"It's okay. I learned a long time ago that you process without me." She pulls away and walks off. I let her, turning to the door, pressing my hands on the wooden surface, chin dropping to my chest, memories pounding at my mind. I did leave because of my father, but I came back because of her. He doesn't get to divide us again. I'm doing a good enough job of that myself. I push off the door and walk into the living room to find Candace back in her chair across from Adam. She doesn't look at me, but Adam damn sure does, arching a brow in question.

I ignore him, walk around the couch, catch Candace's hand, pull her to her feet and then kiss her hard and fast. When I'm done, I sit her back down, walk to my chair, grab my MacBook and sit down next to her on the chair. "Let's talk about the documents I found in your father's office."

She leans in and kisses my cheek and I swear I can feel the ice in this big bad piece of shit assassin's heart melting.

CHAPTER THIRTY-THREE

Candace

The moment Rick walked into the living room after seeing his father, he kissed me, and I'd melted. The minute he'd sat down next to me, closing hours worth of space we'd endured, I'd felt hope. Hope I'd lost last night. Hope that helps me control my anger at his father and my own.

Now, hours later, the rain and early evening hour have darkened the room to the point that the lamps have been flipped on. Adam and Smith sit on the couch with open bags of chips, and a half-empty bottle of whiskey adorns the coffee table. Rick and I lay down in the middle of the floor, exhausted by file after file that does nothing to tell me what turned Gabriel against my father.

"What if it's nothing my father did at all?" I ask, rolling to a sitting position and leaning on one hand to look down at Rick. "Gabriel's running for office. Maybe he just sees my father as a problem."

"I don't buy it," he says. "Marrying you should control your father." He raises up on his elbows. "He thought he was under control. That text message you found says that he no longer believes that to be true."

"Then I have to find the proof we need to take him down and protect my father. I'm close enough to Gabriel to do that. I'm the one who can find what we need." My cellphone rings on the coffee table and my lips purse. "That's going to be him."

"Hand me the phone," Rick suggests. "I need to find out where he wants me to mail his balls when I cut them off."

"That's not funny," I chide.

"It wasn't a joke," he assures me.

I grab my phone, glancing at the screen to confirm Gabriel is my caller, but not before the call drops. "Damn it," I murmur. "I need to call him back." I move to the chair where I was sitting earlier. The ringing begins again and I glance at Rick's handsome, scowling face. "You *know* I have to take it," I say in earnest, and I don't wait for a reply. I answer the call. "Hi," I say, my gaze landing on a bag of Cheetos, while I feel Rick's stare like a sunburn blistering my skin, willing me to look his way. I can't. Not and play this game with Gabriel. "How are things?" I ask him, somehow sounding half normal.

"It's been a long day," Gabriel says, sounding weary. "The threat that came in seems to have amounted to nothing, but we're all here, and the governor wants us to use this as an opportunity for future readiness."

"That seems smart," I say tightly. "Anything you need for me to do here?"

"Just keep being you, honey. How do you feel?"

"Still not grand, but better than last night. It might be good you're gone. It would suck for you to catch this while you're trying to make the world a better place."

"We're going to make the world a better place. You and me together. Get some rest. I'll check on you in the morning."

"When do you think you'll be back?"

"Probably not until at least Tuesday," he says. "I'll let you know. Too long," he adds, softening his voice. "I need to be inside you right now."

My cheeks heat with the idea that Rick is watching me when another man speaks to me in such a way, which feeds my awkward response. "That wouldn't be a good idea considering my present state of health."

"Right," Gabriel says. "Rest. Night." He hangs up.

I lower the phone from my ear.

"What would not be good?" Rick demands, now sitting in the chair by the fireplace again.

I don't look at him. I swallow hard and set my phone down on the table, next to that bag of Cheetos. "He won't be back until Tuesday."

"What the fuck did he say to you, Candace?" Rick snaps.

I force my gaze to his burning blue stare. "It's a game I'm playing, Rick."

"Fuck the game and all of this Walker ethics bullshit," he growls. "I really do need to just kill that motherfucker." He scrubs his jaw, hands settling on his knees before he stands up, and stalks into the kitchen.

Adam starts to get up. I hold up a hand. "I need to talk to him alone."

He nods, but I'm already on my feet, already walking. I find Rick leaning on the counter, his muscular arms crossed in front of his broad chest, that Beret tattoo peeking from under his sleeve, his blue eyes darn near black with anger. And I get it. The idea of him with another woman has destroyed me many a time over the years.

I close the space between us and step in front of him, my hands settling on his arms. "What do you want me to do?"

His lashes lower, his expression all hard lines and shadows, as he murmurs, "I don't fucking know."

"We have to talk about this. We need a plan that we both can live with."

His hands come down on my waist and he pulls me to him. "What did he say to you?"

"I'm not telling you that."

"Did he tell you where he wanted his tongue? Or was it his cock?"

"Stop," I bite out. "Stop doing that. It isn't helping us."

His forehead lowers to mine and he breathes out. "I know you don't know this, but leaving you was hell. Coming back to you wearing another man's ring, ten times worse." Emotion roughens up his voice.

My hand settles on the rough stubble along his jawline. "I don't want him. I want you. Last night—"

"I know. I fucked up." He pulls back to look at me. "We need to get rid of Gabriel."

"We need to reach my father," I say. "He might have the evidence against him we need. Wait. I should go to my father's office and search there. I have clearance because of my military contracts."

"Are you working on a project at Fort Sam?"

"No, but—"

"Then you can't be seen there without him present. It'll look suspicious. But you're right. We need to search his office. I can go."

"How can you go? You don't have clearance."

"My father. I'll meet him there."

"No," I say quickly. "No, Rick. That's nothing but trouble waiting to happen. Please." My hope starts to tilt, a ship in the ocean sinking quickly in the abyss. "He affects you. He affects us."

"He won't affect us." He strokes my hair behind my ear. "I'm not the man I was when I left." He pulls me closer and kisses me. "I need to do this for me and for us. And it makes sense that your father would keep anything he has on Gabriel in his office."

"If I need to put the ring back on, I will. It means nothing."

"Except that he has the right to fuck you? No. He's not fucking you. He's not kissing you. He's not putting his piece of shit hands on you. I'm going to search the office. And one way or another, I will be returning that ring to Gabriel and personally shoving it up his ass."

"I have to protect my father."

"*We* have to protect your father. And that's exactly what I'm doing by acting now, not later." He kisses me and sets me away from him, before walking toward the living room.

And with my heart thundering in my chest, I rush after him, catching up with him in the living room, just in time for me to hear him explaining his plan to Adam and Smith. Just in time to hear them agree that it's a good plan. I can't stop this from happening. He's going to go see the man who has always made him feel like a monster. And the thing about believing you're a monster or anything for that matter is that you try to live up to the expectations.

CHAPTER THIRTY-FOUR

Savage

I claim the chair by the couch while Smith fills a glass of whiskey and shoves it in my direction. I shove it away and with good reason. Booze, me, and my father are a bad mix. "I need my father's phone number."

Adam arches a brow. "You don't know your father's phone number?"

I scowl. "Just call Asher and have him hack the damn number. I need to do this now, tonight."

"I have it," Candace says, stepping into the living room, "but this is not a good idea." She rounds the couch and looks at Adam. "He and his father are like a volcanic eruption about to happen."

"You and him—that's a volcanic eruption about to happen," Adam replies.

"That remark serves what purpose?" she challenges.

I snatch the phone from her hand. "Why do you have his number?"

"I always had his number," she says. "Unlike you, I didn't delete it." She cuts her stare and then looks at me again. "It was the only connection I had left to you. Or he was."

She held onto me, even when I was certain she'd let go. That knowledge grinds through me and fills my black soul with regrets a black soul shouldn't be able to feel. "I can handle my father, baby. I promise." I tug her down to sit next to me, kissing her temple before I tab through her phone, find my father's number, and dial. He answers on the first ring.

"Candace," he greets. "This is a surprise."

"It's not Candace," I say. "How about a surgical match-up father? Military lab in an hour? We'll match scalpels."

"I'll have a pass waiting for you at security. See you soon, son." He disconnects.

Son.

Fuck.

That word from that man makes me want to shoot someone, someone like him.

Candace catches my hand. "Rick?"

I glance down at her and kiss her. "I'm good."

"Matching scalpels with your father? That's good? Are you even licensed to operate?"

"Yes," I say. "The military made sure of it and Walker maintained my provisional licensing for our special operations. And no, I will never go into private practice. That's never going to happen." I don't look at her when I say that. I can't get in my own head, or hers right now, about where we once talked about our future taking me and us. "This is a go," I say to the room, changing the topic.

"I'll ride shotgun," Adam offers.

"And I'll stay with Candace," Smith chimes in.

"I didn't think I was in danger," Candace objects. "Go with Rick."

"Better safe than sorry," I say. "He needs to stay with you." I hand her phone to Smith. "I need you to put everyone she might ever need in there and make sure she knows who they are."

He takes the phone and eyes Candace. "This will take me about fifteen minutes. It's a lot of numbers."

"My phone," Candace says.

"You want me to make you a list and you can put in the numbers?" Smith offers, holding it out to her.

"No," she says. "That's not it." She turns to me. "I can't believe I forgot to tell you this. I snuck into Gabriel's offices before the party. His door was locked and I couldn't get in, but I took random photos of documents in his secretary's desk." She glances at Smith. "They're in my photos for your review." She returns her attention to me. "You should search

176

his campaign manager's house. I hid under her desk when he came into the offices with her, and apparently, she's his best fuck and I'm his arm candy."

"Holy fuck," I murmur, catching her to me, blown away by the fact that she knew and endured that crap to protect her father. "Baby, I'm sorry."

"Are you?"

"Yes." I cup her face. "It felt bad. I know it felt bad."

"Understanding from a cold-blooded killer? What's wrong with you?"

"Don't glamorize who or what I am, baby. That's not good for either of us." I kiss her and release her. "Smith—"

"I'll go search her place," he confirms.

Adam looks at Candace. "We have a man watching the street."

"How many of you are there?" she asks.

"They're like gnats that multiply every time I tell them to stay out of this," I say.

Adam stands up. "I'll meet you in the car," he says. "I'm going to alert the gnats about the plan."

"I'm going to get these numbers in Candace's phone and shoot these photos to Asher before I leave," Smith says.

Adam disappears out of the room and I push to my feet, taking Candace with me. "Walk me out." I catch her hand and lead her into the kitchen, but once we're at the garage door, I turn and fold her close. "I won't be long."

"I don't want you to go."

"I need to do this."

She grabs my shirt. "I feel like you're going to walk out of that door, face your father, and never come back."

"That's not going to happen."

"Your father fucks with your head. We don't need that."

"I told you—"

"I slept alone last night, Rick, when we could have been together. That's how quick you are to decide that you're the killer who doesn't belong in my bed."

There's a complicated history there of me wanting her and deciding she was better off without me that words won't erase. But I try. I have to try. "I already told you, the minute

I saw you again, I wasn't walking away, no matter what kind of selfish bastard that makes me." I kiss her long and deep. "You won't be sleeping alone tonight." I lean in, inhaling her sweet floral scent and then force myself to set her away from me—one of the hardest fucking things I've ever done, and I've done some really hard fucking things in my life—and I exit to the garage.

CHAPTER THIRTY-FIVE

Candace

I fight tears when that door shuts behind Rick.

I fight tears because Smith is here and I can't let them fall. I fight tears because the last time that Rick and his father performed surgery was all about death. It was the night his mother died, only four days after he'd lost a patient on the table. A patient he'd felt his father had caused to die. Rick was gone less than a month later. Rick's father didn't control his deployment, but the events of that night, made him welcome it. Rick didn't admit that to me, but I felt it. I felt it in every pore of my existence. And there's no way his state of mind, when he left, didn't affect who he became after he left.

"You okay?"

I turn to find Smith standing in the doorway. "Yes," I lie. "Did you look at the photos?"

"Not yet. Why don't you help me?"

"Don't you need to go search Gabriel's side chick's house?"

He arches a brow. "Side Chick?"

"Monica. His campaign manager who I really wish would wrap her legs around him and hold on tight. If she wants to break his back while she's at it, that would work just fine, but at the very least, hold on, and don't let go. Keep him away from me."

He laughs. "It's almost as if you're speaking from Savage's lips. I get glimpses of why you're so damn good with Rick. I need to wait until later in the evening when the neighborhood goes to sleep."

The remark about me being so good with Rick cuts. He left me behind. It's hard to get past that. He didn't just leave, he stayed away for a very long time. "I'll make coffee." I walk to the pot and get busy, the one thing that's kept me sane over the years.

Once I push the brew button, I turn to find Smith settling at the kitchen table, a MacBook in front of him. "I've loaded all the photos for you for easy access," he says, turning the screen towards an empty seat. "And I've got them on my screen as well as sending them to Asher, who is our next best hacker to Blake. He'll cross-reference keywords he finds to Gabriel and your father."

I join him and sit down as he opens another MacBook in front of him. "The operation seems quite sophisticated."

"It is," he says, glancing at me. "We're the best of the best. That includes Savage," he says. "All that big talk and the stupid jokes fade away when you're depending on him. He comes through. Always."

"Were you there when he saved Adam?"

"I wasn't, but I did a mission with him that was rough. That man is a beast of a warrior."

"It's in his blood."

"Don't read into that. It doesn't mean he's walking away from you again. About half of our staff is married."

Married.

To Rick.

That very idea feels impossible and therefore I don't comment. I start tabbing through the photos I took again just to be sure there's nothing important there and it's not long before we both nurse cups of coffee. "Rain stopped," Smith says. "Talk about a downpour."

"It's supposed to start again," I say because I looked at my weather app earlier. "I'm sure that doesn't make the break-in easy."

"It's messy, but it also keeps the neighbors inside." He studies me. "He's different with you. Softer. It's good. He needs you."

"Until his father convinces him he's such a monster, that I deserve better."

"You think his father's that bad?"

"I know he is." I stand up and walk to the coffee pot to refill my mug, fighting back memories that will only make this night longer. I'm not letting myself travel back to the past. I need to stay here and rooted in the present. I just hope Rick can do the same.

Savage

I drop Adam at his car a few blocks from the house and head toward Fort Sam, and at least for now, the rain has slowed to nothing. The past pounds at my mind, flashes of that shit night when I lost my mother, torment me in a way I've suppressed for years now. I hit the highway, pushing the Porsche to its limits, the events leading up to that night, dominating my thoughts now. I try to picture my mother again and the very fact that I can't, presses my speed. She was pretty and sweet, I know that much, and she loved Candace. An image of her in the kitchen with Candace baking Christmas cookies and laughing while I watched, is ruined by the memory of my father coming home and acting like the ass he'd been since his accident.

"A fool in the kitchen, trying not to look like a fool outside the kitchen," he'd said. "I won't eat those things."

She'd burst into tears and I'd have beaten his ass if she and Candace hadn't grabbed my arms and held on.

That was a week before my mother died on Christmas Eve.

I cut off the road and idle in the emergency lane, willing myself not to go where I'm about to go, right before I see my father. I'm not fucking do it. I grab my phone and I start to dial Candace, the way I have a million times over the years, but I stop myself. She's worried about the collision course that has always been me and my father. I'm going to make it worse. I drop my phone into the seat and pull back onto the highway, cranking the radio while accelerating and pushing the car again. I don't ease up until I'm at the base.

Pulling up to the security gate, I'm cleared for entry, and I drive to the medical building, where I park the car and kill the engine. But I don't get out. I grip the steering wheel and squeeze my eyes shut and I can't stop what follows. I'm back in the past, back to that fucking day. I was here, right here, at this building. Candace had been at my parents' house with my mom. My cellphone had rung and the display lit up with her name. I can still remember her call like it was yesterday. I'm there now, answering Candace's call.

"Hey, baby."

"Rick," she'd breathes out, her voice a raspy tremble. "I need to see you right now."

"What is it?"

"I'm here. It's important." Her voice hitches and then firms. "I'm in the staff break room. Come here now."

"I have a meeting, baby. Give me half an hour."

"Now, Rick. Now." She hangs up.

The hang up is what gets me. It stuns me. Adrenaline surges through me, pulsing and throbbing. I start walking, my steps fast but steady, the short journey seemingly eternal. At the staff lounge, I enter to find Candace alone, her face streaked with makeup, eyes puffy. The minute her gaze meets mine, tears pour down her cheeks.

She rushes toward me and I step into her, catching her arms. "What is it? What happened?"

"I went shopping with your mom. We had fun. We were laughing and—and your dad came home right after we got back. He was upset." She sobs and already anger burns in my gut. He can't just stop. "He yelled at her and then he shoved her, Rick. He even hit her."

The anger of moments before is now a roar. "That bastard. I'm going to kill him." I try to pull away and she grabs me. "No," she orders urgently. "No, you need to listen to me. Please. Please. Listen."

"I am, but—"

"He left to come here, to come to work, but she wasn't better when he was gone, Rick. Her chest started hurting."

A cold foreboding freezes my anger. "Where is she? Is she okay?"

She shakes her head. "No. No, Rick. She's not okay." She wraps her arms around me, holds me tight. "Baby, she had a massive heart attack and she didn't make it. They couldn't—"

"Stop. Don't say it. I can't hear you say it. I can't." My voice is calm, almost distant, and the cold is colder now, too, ice slowing encasing my heart. "Where is she now?"

"They took her to Memorial Hospital," she says, her fingers curling on my cheek. "But she's gone, baby."

She's gone.

She can't be gone.

The door opens behind me.

"There you are, son."

At the sound of my father's voice, the cold becomes heat, it becomes anger. I catch Candace's arms again, to set her away from me. She grabs my scrub top. "Rick, no. Whatever you're about to do, don't. He clearly doesn't know yet. Let me—"

"Son," he says.

That's all it takes to push me over the edge. She's dead and the last thing she knew was his abuse. I set Candace firmly away from me, turn around and snap. I do what I wanted to do a week ago when he yelled at her, and four days ago again, when he caused a patient to die on my table. I do what I should have already done, too fucking long ago. I launch myself at him, shove him against the wall and start beating him.

I blink back to the present and remember being pulled off of him. He'd been hurt. I'd been glad. Hurt badly enough to miss my mom's funeral. He didn't deserve to be there anyway. I'd endured the military review over my actions and when they'd wanted to put me back in an operating room, I didn't feel ready. Candace's father had suggested I deploy under a special program he operated. I'd said yes that day because I wanted to kill my father and I feared I might do it. I'd felt myself changing, turning into a killer. And that's what happened. I'd become a killer but one with the control I didn't have that day I'd attacked my father. He doesn't have the control over me he once did.

I open the car door and get out. Let the reunion begin and be the fuck over with, not fucking soon enough.

CHAPTER THIRTY-SIX

Candace

"Well, this was a dead-end," I say, finishing up the review of the documents I'd photographed.

"All is not lost yet," Smith says. "Asher is working on the cross-references in between monitoring your piece of shit fiancé." He eyes my finger. "Don't you have a ring?"

"Rick took it."

He laughs. "Figures." He glances at his watch. "It's about that time. I'm heading out."

"If I want to leave, can I?"

"To go where?"

"I don't know. The store. A coffee shop. I just don't want to be here right now."

"Our guy is watching the house. He'll give you backup wherever you go."

"But I'm not in danger?"

"We're just being cautious. We Walkers guard family like they're gold. And you're family, even if you don't know it yet. I won't come back when I'm done, but I'll text you if I find anything. I figure you and Savage need some time alone."

"Thanks, Smith."

"New friend. That's me. Remember that."

I offer a weak smile and he disappears into the garage. I have no idea what car he's taking or how he's traveling, and I don't care. He's resourceful. I stand up and walk into the bedroom, entering the closet where I push to my toes and grab a red leather box off the top shelf. Carrying it to the bed, I sit down on the mattress and open the lid. Inside are the letters Rick wrote to me while he was deployed but only one really matters. The last one. I haven't dared look at it in years but with shaky hands, I remove the handwritten letter from the envelope, unfold it, and read:

Candace:

I love you. I will always love you. And that's why I can't bring this hell back to you. Ever. The idea of never touching you or kissing you again kills me. Destroys me. But I know now that death is a part of me like it is my father. I can't do to you what he did to my mother. I won't forget you. I hope you do me.

Love forever,

Rick

My throat is thick with emotion. My heart hurts. I hurt. Again. I hurt again. My mind travels back to the day I received it. Like I did every day, I anxiously checked the mailbox, relieved and excited to find his words waiting on me. And like I did with every letter, I made coffee, sat down on the porch he built us, and opened it. The day this letter came, I'd been sick, running a fever, alone at home. I'd read those words and dropped the scalding hot tea I was drinking all over me. And then I'd cried like I'm about to now.

"Damn it," I murmur. "Why am I doing this to myself?" But I know. I know why. Because I think he's already gone again and I'm not sure I'm going to survive it this time.

Still, I torture myself further. I stick the letter back in the envelope and trade the envelope for the black velvet ring box also inside the box. With my breath lodged in my throat, I open it, staring down at the sapphire and diamond engagement ring that Rick had given me six months after we met. It's simple but beautiful. It's perfect. We were perfect, or so I thought. I shut the lid and stick the ring back in the box, before sealing the lid. It's impossible to do though without traveling back to the night he deployed. He'd stood on my doorstep, his hands on my face. "I'll be back. And when I am, we're getting married. I love you, baby. More than I thought it was possible to love." And then he'd kissed me before walking away for eight long years.

CHAPTER THIRTY-SEVEN

Savage

With a field bag at my hip, I walk into the hospital to find my father waiting on me at the door. I wait for the moment, when memories crash over me, and I want to beat him again. It doesn't come. He just doesn't seem worth it anymore. "You really came," he says and there's a light in his eyes, a sense of achievement like he has me. Like he owns me.

"Not for the reasons you think," I say. "I need something and you owe me."

His eyes narrow. "I owe you? Really? I haven't see you in eight years. What do I owe you for?"

"It amuses me that he really doesn't get how quickly I could snap his neck and he'd be over.

"You're still alive. *You* owe *me* for letting that happen."

He smirks, and it's sad to see such a brilliant man, fades into this kind of stupidity. "You want something from me. What do I get in return?"

"The part where I said you owed me? You don't understand that? Or you don't care?"

"Boy, I brought you into this world," he says. "You want something from me, you give me something. You and me at an operating table. That's what you said you were coming here to give me. I get what I want. You get what you want."

"You really think you and me and a cadaver is a good reunion?"

"I've heard stories of your skill," he says. "An old man wants to see his boy in action."

187

"I assure you, pops, you do not want a demonstration of my skills. I told you. I'm not here for you." I step around him and start walking. "Let's go," I order over my shoulder.

He falls into step beside me. "I'll bite. Why are you here? What do you want?"

"To see my father," I say. "And if you ever want me to give you that match-up over the operating table, that's your story."

"On one condition."

I give him a side eye. "I thought we just set the condition."

"One more."

"Of course," I bite out, cutting my stare. "What condition?"

"You have coffee with me."

I stop at an elevator and he scans his badge before I punch the call button and ask, "Why would I do that, old man?"

"It buys you my silence."

He wants something. That's why he came to the house today. Not to see me but because he wants something. "When?"

The doors to the elevator open and we both step inside. He punches the button to his floor. "Tonight," he says.

"Not tonight."

"Tomorrow, then," he counters.

"Fine. Tomorrow. I suggest a public place. It's in your best interest."

"I do believe that you've taught me that lesson well. Beat it into me in fact." There's bitterness in those words, that warn of where his head is right now. He wants something alright—revenge.

Whatever, fucktard, I think, and when the car opens, I exit and start walking. He falls into step beside me, a brilliant surgeon who's a lousy man. At least he puts those brains to use by following my lead and keeping his mouth shut.

Twenty minutes later, we've taken a long path to another building without human encounter, and he's opened the general's door for me. I step inside and he says, "See you tomorrow." He then shuts me inside and disappears.

I don't know or care what he wants. Not right now. I scan the office. "What do you have on Gabriel, General? Get your office talking to me before you end up dead." I walk around the desk and sit down, and when the drawers won't open, I reach into my pocket, pull out a tool I keep handy, and I quickly pop the lock. I start taking photos, lots of fucking photos, the likes of which could be considered criminal since they're of U.S. government property. But I've killed for our government. They can share some photos. The problem is none of any of this feels relevant, but coding and hidden messages happen. Often.

I do another scan of the room and this time my gaze lands on a bookshelf. I lock the desk back up and head in that direction, surveying books, looking for something that might hold a secret I need. Nothing feels right. I sit down on the couch and reach underneath, and bingo, I hit something. I grab what turns out to be a familiar military training manual. I flip it open, shutting it again when it appears uneventful, before sliding it back where I found it. I'm about to move on when something hits me, something I've seen once before.

Pulling the book back out, I open it again. Midway through, the binding is cut and inside there appears to be documents that aren't coming out without destroying the book. That's enough for me. Too much time has passed for comfort. I shut the book, shove it into my field bag, along with a few other suspect items, and it's time to get the hell out of Dodge before I get caught.

At the door, I slowly open it, and once I'm certain that my path is clear, I exit into the hallway. I start walking and I don't even think about looking for my father. I'm carrying top-secret military documents in my bag. Now is not the time to reminisce about his many levels of dickheadedness.

I walk, slow and confident, toward the exit. I'm about ten feet from the door when I hear a bellowing, "Stop right there."

And I know the minute I hear that voice that I'm not getting out of here without kicking someone's ass.

CHAPTER THIRTY-EIGHT

Candace

An hour after Smith leaves to search Monica's house, I'm climbing the walls. I've cleaned up the mess three big men created. I've read through more files. I've paced. I've drunk coffee. I've replayed the night Rick's mother died in my head and that's the last time he saw his father with excruciating detail. I want to text or call him, but I resist with grand effort. If he's sneaking around and searching my father's office, sound might not be good. I have to wait on him. I have to wait and he might not ever return. Finally, I can't take it anymore. Smith approved me leaving should I wish to do so, and I wish to do so. I need out of this house. I grab my purse and slip on a rain jacket, making my way to the garage. Once I'm there, I know exactly where I'm going. I head out into the rainy night, and there is no hesitation in my acceleration.

Fifteen minutes later, nearly ten-thirty at this point, I pull up in front of the coffee bar where I met Rick all those years ago and did so in the middle of a downpour, much like this one. Ironically, I manage to park in the exact spot I was in that night. The very spot that helped launch the beginning of something wonderful and I really need to believe that's where Rick and I are at again. I grab my briefcase with my sketchpad inside, open my door and my umbrella, and in a flash, I'm inside the coffee bar. I drop my dripping umbrella by the door, hang up my wet rain jacket on a rack, and then scan the sparsely occupied seating areas. Choosing a window spot, I set my things down and then rush to the counter. I order a coffee and a chocolate cake, recreating what was a wonderful night years before. I need that hope. I really do.

A few minutes later, I'm settled in and watching it rain, my sketchpad for the project I'm working on in front of me. I've also got coffee and chocolate cake. An hour later, I've still not heard from Rick. I haven't even heard from Smith, not that he promised to check-in. At this point, I'm on coffee number two, my design work sucks, and I haven't touched my cake. I just need to pee because, why wouldn't I? I've drunk a ton of coffee today. Feeling anxious and emotional, I grab my purse and make a path in that direction. After finding the downstairs bathroom locked, I head up the stairs to the upper level. Once I'm down a hallway in the one-person bathroom, I do what I came for, wash up, and then catch the edge of the counter, staring at myself in the mirror. And I look pathetic, a woman who would do anything for a man who has proven he doesn't want her, not beyond a moment.

"He's not coming back," I say, trying to give myself a pep talk, that doesn't feel like a pep talk at all. "You know this," I add, trying harder. "You knew the minute he went to see his father. You've survived this before. You can do it now." My chin drops to my chest. I don't think I'm going to survive it. My father's in danger. Rick's gone. I need to go home. I can meltdown there.

Straightening, I smooth my hair and damn it, I check my silent phone again before shoving the stupid thing back in my purse now at my hip. I draw a deep breath and open the door only to gasp.

Rick is standing there, looking big and savage, so very savage. So very him. "Hey, baby," he says, his arm on the frame above his head. "Miss me?"

I don't even try to play it coy. I fling myself forward and wrap my arms around him, pressing my head to his thundering heart. "Hey," he says softly, catching my head and tilting my gaze to his, studying me. "You really didn't think I was coming back, did you?"

"I know what your father does to you."

"I've seen too much and been too many hellish places to let that man rattle me anymore, but he tried. He also failed."

"He failed?"

"Yes, baby. He failed. I'll tell you about it over coffee and cake."

"I'd like that, but, Rick, I need to know—I mean—last night—"

"I told you. I fucked up. I'm not going to make that mistake again." He leans in and kisses me, a deep, melt-me-right-out-of-my-shoes kind of kiss and by the time it's over, we're in the bathroom and he's shutting the door.

"Rick, what if someone catches us?"

"The great thing about being with a man like me, baby, is I'll just kill anyone that gets in our way."

"Are you trying to scare me away?"

"Yes, and I hope like hell it doesn't work." His hands go to my waist. "Baby, I am who I am. I own it. I can't be anyone else."

"Good. Own it. Please own it, because when you don't, last night happens."

He cups my backside. "Oh well. I think maybe me being a bit rough turns you on. You do like it a little rough. Maybe I'll spank that pretty little ass right here."

"No." I catch his shirt in my hand. "No. Do not even think about it. You will do no such thing."

"Oh come on, baby. Remember that one time—"

"No, Rick. Not here."

He laughs low and wicked. "I'll behave, but let's not go home yet. Let's have that coffee and chocolate cake. It's been a long time since we did this."

He's referencing how this became our place. We'd come here, we'd work and talk, and repeat. It was special.

"I'd like that."

"Good, because it's been too long."

He strokes my hair again, a familiar action that I didn't realize until now I missed terribly. He was always touching me, always tender, a man I always knew had a dark side. But I also knew that part of him was one part of a complex, wonderful man. A man who just happens to have become a surgeon and an assassin. Point made.

There is so much more to Rick Savage than meets the eye. I always knew that about him. I always loved that about him. I need to make sure he knows that, too. Now. Tonight. There is so much that needs to be said between us. Now. Tonight.

CHAPTER THIRTY-NINE

Savage

Sitting with Candace, sharing coffee, cake, and conversation, I am, perhaps the most human I've been in eight years, right here, right now. "Did you search my father's office? And did you find anything?"

"I did and yes. A book with something hidden inside."

"What was it?"

"I saved it for you and me to look at together. He's your father. I thought—"

"Thank you. Thank *you*, Rick." Her voice is low, affected. "There you go being a killer with a sensitive side again."

The compliment punches me in the gut and I lean forward and grab her hands. "Baby, I'm terrified every time you turn me into a hero. I'm *not* a hero."

"Yes, you are. And you know what? Until you see yourself that way, there will always be another last night. Or at least, until you stop calling yourself a killer. And I need to, too."

"No. No, you don't. Because I need to know you see me clearly. I need to know that you aren't going to wake up next to me one morning and freak the fuck out."

"Waking up next to you, and then having you leave again, that is what will freak me the fuck out. I can't go through that, Rick. So if that's what's going to happen, step back now."

"I'm not stepping back. I'm stepping close. And I'm holding onto you this time."

She reaches over the table and traces my goatee, searching my face. "I'm trusting you with my heart, Rick Savage."

"And I will guard it with my own."

Her eyes search mine, her fingers stroking the scar on my cheek. I catch her hand. "Does it bother you?"

"No. I'd call it sexy if I didn't know it a war wound. Tell me that story."

I pull back, my hands going to my knees, gaze sliding left, memories ripping through me that I smash. "I've seen and done things that I can't make go away. You know that, right?"

"Yes," she says, no hesitation in her reply. "I know."

"That's all I was for a while—those things. You remind me that there's something more. That *I'm* something more."

"What happened with your father?" she asks, the topic of me being more, taking her there. Of course, it takes her there. No one knows better than her how low my father took me.

"I declined his request that we match scalpels. He took me to your father's office with a little too much willingness. He even invited me for coffee."

Her eyes go wide. "Your father? He invited you for coffee? I'm confused."

"Yeah, I know, right? He wants something. I don't know what. I doubt I'll give him the chance to tell me. I would have been back sooner, but the chief of staff, right along with my father, cornered me. Tried to recruit me back."

"And you said what?"

"I declined."

Relief washes over her face. "Good, because—"

"You don't have to say it. I know. The Army divided us, baby. The Army doesn't bring us back together." My phone buzzes with a text. I glance down and read it before setting it aside. "Not much at the bimbo Monica's house."

She laughs that perfect laugh of hers. "You are still so you."

"Am I?"

"Yes. You are. The things that come out of your mouth. I love the way you are."

Heat expands between us, damn near catching me on fire. "Show me. At home, naked."

"At home?" she challenges.

I stand and pull her to her feet in front of me. "The only home I've ever had, Candace, is you."

"Rick," she whispers, her eyes tearing up because I'm the fucking bastard that made those words emotional, painful even. It's time to make them mean something right and real.

I grab her bag and slide it onto her shoulder, guiding her to the front door where I slip on my coat, and then help her into hers. We step outside into a light drizzle and she laughs at the sight of my car, parked next to hers. "Did you really block my door?"

"Just like old times, right?"

She smiles and pushes to her toes, intending to give me a quick kiss. I'm not having it. I catch her to me, and drink her in long and deep before I say, "I love you, Candace. I have always loved you. I'm going to make you love me again."

"I already love you, Rick. I never stopped. So don't crush my heart again."

"I told you. I'll protect it with my own, baby." I kiss her quick and hard this time. "Let's go *home*. In the same car. I don't want to split up. I'll get your car in the morning."

"Yes," she says. "Yes that's good."

"I'll pull out so you can get in."

She nods and I jog to my door, climb inside the vehicle and quickly start the engine to an appropriate Porsche roar. Once it's live and ready, I back up and place the engine in idle. The rain starts to pound down again and Candace runs for the Porsche. I'm there when she gets there, holding the door open for her. I might be the bastard you don't want to see at the end of your bed holding a knife, but I have manners. Once she's sealed safely inside, I join her, and yes, I kiss her again, because fuck, I can't stop kissing her. I don't even want to try.

197

I then rev the engine and crank the radio to Jason Aldean's Lights Come On. She laughs and in another few minutes, we're on the highway, my mood completely different than it was on the way to see my father. I'm with Candace. I'm home. I'm where I belong. The world is right until I glance up and start noticing lights in the rearview mirror, my Spidey senses on alert. I change lanes and slow down. The other car changes lanes and slows down. I exit down a winding road that I used to know well. They exit.

"Why are we exiting?" Candace asks.

I turn down the radio and open the glove box where a gun rests. "You still know how to use that?"

"Yes. Oh God. What is it?" She glances back at the lights and then to me once more. "Who is it?"

I pull my gun I'd left under the seat and set it on my lap. "We're about to find out. Hold on." We're going to take them for a fast, hard ride. I accelerate and Candace grabs the gun, then the roof, as I cut right, left, right again, turn down a narrow road, then back onto the main road. "Gabriel knows, doesn't he? He knows."

"That I'm here to kill him? Maybe."

"You're not here to kill him."

"Oh, I am, baby. I'm going to kill that bastard. Hold on!" I do a one-eighty and when the other car skids to the side of the road, I slam the gear into idle. "Get on the floorboard."

Candace does as I say, sliding off her seat. "What are you going to do?"

"Handle this so we can get on with our night." I unhook my belt. "Do you think pizza again after this is too much pizza? It is, right?"

"Rick!" Candace yells at me. "We're about to die and you're talking about pizza?"

"Right. Sorry, baby. Killing people makes me hungry. And we aren't about to die. Someone else is." I wait until the other driver opens his door and then, and only then, when he's exposed, do I open mine.

It's time.

Party time.

THE END...FOR NOW

Readers,

I hope you're loving Savage and Candace's story so far! I can't wait to share their next installment, SAVAGE BURN, on February 25th – it's available for pre-order everywhere. I would love to hear what you thought of the launch of Savage's trilogy! Be sure to reach out: @AuthorLisaReneeJones on Facebook and @LisaReneeJones on Instagram and Twitter.

GET THE NEXT BOOK IN THE SAVAGE TRILOGY

https://savagetrilogy.weebly.com/

What's next for me? DIRTY RICH BETRAYAL: LOVE ME FOREVER (Grayson & Mia's wedding book) is coming soon, and of course Savage's story continues with SAVAGE BURN and SAVAGE LOVE! Check out that, plus an all-new trilogy coming mid-late 2020!

https://lisareneejonescomingsoon.weebly.com/

Don't forget, if you want to be the first to know about upcoming books, giveaways, sales and any other exciting news I have to share please be sure you're signed up for my newsletter! As an added bonus everyone receives a free ebook when they sign-up!

http://lisareneejones.com/newsletter-sign-up/

WALKER SECURITY

Did you fall in love with the Walker men? Three of them already have their own standalone books and they're available now in ebook, print, and audio!

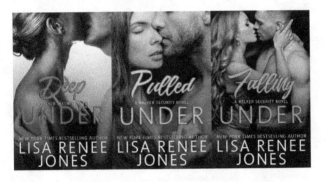

Lethal, alpha, and ready. These are the men of Walker Security. Recruited by the founding Walker brothers for their elite status and skill in a branch of military or law enforcement, the Walker men fight hard and love harder. They live by a code of honor, and fight for right over wrong. And they will do whatever it takes to protect the innocent and defeat the enemy. These are the stories of these elite Walker men and the women who bring them to their knees.

LEARN MORE AND BUY HERE:

https://walkersecurity.weebly.com/

GRAYSON BENNETT'S STORY!

DIRTY RICH BETRAYAL—AVAILABLE EVERYWHERE NOW

DIRTY RICH BETRAYAL: LOVE ME FOREVER—AVAILABLE FOR PRE-ORDER EVERYWHERE. THIS IS GOING TO BE AN APPLE BOOKS EXCLSUIVE, WHICH WILL PUBLISH THERE ON JANUARY 14TH AND WILL PUBLISH EVERYWHERE ELSE ON MAY 12TH!

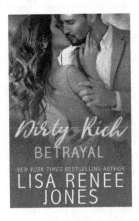 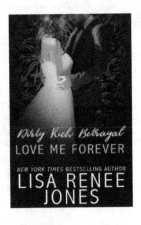

EXCERPT FROM DIRTY RICH BETRAYAL

He kisses me, a quick brush of lips over lips. "I need you naked. I need to feel you next to me." He rolls me to my back and with that "for now" in the air, he moves and resettles with his lips to my stomach and this is not an accidental connection. My heart squeezes with the certainty that he's reminding me of how many times he told me he wanted a little girl just like me. It affects me. We had so many plans. We were best friends. We were so many things that happened so very quickly and easily, and then it was gone.

He pulls down my pants, and all too quickly my sneakers and everything else are gone. I'm naked and not just my body. I am so very naked with this man and always have been. But as for my body, I'm not alone for long. He strips away his clothes, and I lift to my elbows to admire all that sinewy, perfect muscle before he reaches down, grabs my legs and pulls me to him. The minute my backside is on the edge of the bed, he goes down on a knee. I sit up and cup his face. "Not now. Now I need—I need—"

He cups my head and pulls my mouth to his, kissing me with a long stroke of his tongue before he says, "And I need to taste you."

"Not now. I'm not leaving. We have time. I need—you. Here with me."

His eyes soften but he still leans in and licks my clit, and then suckles. I'm all but undone by the sensation because one thing I know and know well is how good this man is with his tongue. But he doesn't ignore my request. He pushes off the floor, and in a heartbeat, he's kissing me and I don't even know how we end up in the center of the bed, our naked bodies entwined. We just are and it's wonderful and right in ways nothing has been in so very long.

He lifts my leg to his thigh and presses his thick erection inside me, filling me in ways that go beyond our bodies; driving deep, his hand on my backside, pulling me into him, pushing into me, but then we don't move. Then we just lay there, intimately connected, lost in the moment and each other. "Is this what you wanted?"

"Yes," I say. "This is what I wanted."

"I didn't think I'd ever have you here, like this, with me again."

"Me either," I whisper, my fingers curling on his jaw. "Grayson," I say for no reason other than I need his name on my lips. I need everything with this man.

He kisses me, a fast, deep, passionate kiss. "I missed the hell out of you, Mia. So *fucking* much. I don't think you really understand how much."

This moment, right here, right now, is one of our raw, honest, perfect moments that has always made his betrayal hard to accept. I need that honesty in my life and with him and I don't even think about denying him my truth. "I missed you, too. More than you know, Grayson."

He squeezes my backside and drives into me again. I pant with the sensations that rip through my body, my hand going to his shoulder. "Nothing was right without you," he says. "Nothing, Mia." He kisses me, and I sink into the connection, pressing into him, into his thrust, into the hard warmth of his entire body. Needing to be close. Needing the things that separated us not to exist.

LEARN MORE AND BUY HERE:

https://dirtyrich.weebly.com/dirty-rich-betrayal.html

ALSO BY LISA RENEE JONES

THE INSIDE OUT SERIES

If I Were You
Being Me
Revealing Us
*His Secrets**
Rebecca's Lost Journals
*The Master Undone**
*My Hunger**
No In Between
*My Control**
I Belong to You
*All of Me**

THE SECRET LIFE OF AMY BENSEN

Escaping Reality
Infinite Possibilities
Forsaken
*Unbroken**

CARELESS WHISPERS

Denial
Demand
Surrender

WHITE LIES

Provocative
Shameless

TALL, DARK & DEADLY

Hot Secrets
Dangerous Secrets
Beneath the Secrets

WALKER SECURITY

Deep Under
Pulled Under
Falling Under

LILAH LOVE

Murder Notes
Murder Girl
Love Me Dead
Love Kills

DIRTY RICH

Dirty Rich One Night Stand
Dirty Rich Cinderella Story
Dirty Rich Obsession
Dirty Rich Betrayal
Dirty Rich Cinderella Story: Ever After
Dirty Rich One Night Stand: Two Years Later
Dirty Rich Obsession: All Mine
Dirty Rich Betrayal: Love Me Forever

THE FILTHY TRILOGY

The Bastard
The Princess
The Empire

THE NAKED TRILOGY

One Man

One Woman
Two Together

THE SAVAGE TRILOGY

Savage Hunger
Savage Burn (February 2020)
Savage Love (April 2020)

THE BRILLIANCE TRILOGY

A Reckless Note (June 2020)
A Wicked Song (August 2020)
A Sinful Encore (September 2020)

ABOUT THE AUTHOR

New York Times and USA Today bestselling author Lisa Renee Jones is the author of the highly acclaimed INSIDE OUT series.

In addition to the success of Lisa's INSIDE OUT series, she has published many successful titles. The TALL, DARK AND DEADLY series and THE SECRET LIFE OF AMY BENSEN series, both spent several months on a combination of the New York Times and USA Today bestselling lists. Lisa is also the author of the bestselling LILAH LOVE and WHITE LIES series.

Prior to publishing, Lisa owned multi-state staffing agency that was recognized many times by The Austin Business Journal and also praised by the Dallas Women's Magazine. In 1998 Lisa was listed as the #7 growing women owned business in Entrepreneur Magazine.

Lisa loves to hear from her readers. You can reach her on Twitter and Facebook daily.